MW01235711

Mersey Boys

3rd Edition

By Steven G. Farrell

Edited by Jeanne Putnam and Jennifer Mathews

Celtic-Badger Publishers

Greenville, South Carolina

www.celtic-badger.com

2013

Mersey Boys is dedicated to Joanna Pickering, a beautiful and talented British actress, who shall be forever Ginny Browne in my mind, heart and soul. Keep on rocking, gentle lady.

Author's Note

Mersey Boys is a novel based upon the career of the Beatles. The character of Al Moran never existed in reality therefore his interaction with the Beatles never took place except in my imagination. However, many of the events described in this book actually happened. The legend of the Beatles is well known throughout the world. *Mersey Boys* is just another version of the truth.

—Steven G. Farrell

February 4, 2009

Dear Uncle Adam;

Uncle Al passed away in his sleep less than two hours ago. He had been anticipating his death these past few weeks, so he did me the courtesy of making all the necessary arrangements before I arrived here in England. There isn't much for me to do but to make a few phone calls. I have already contacted his parish priest and the undertaker. I must confess that I am happy that the old boy had his financial house in order and there won't be any hassles in dealing with his estate. He was wealthier than I had expected. The two of us spent the last few days of his life sorting through his things. Whew! You wouldn't believe all the junk he had me throw away. You know how Uncle Al liked to collect odd things, especially books, records and newspaper clippings. He also put into my hand a stack of black and white photographs dating back to the late fifties and early sixties. Wait until you get a load of some of the people in the pictures. His place was literally a museum. He was alert enough to put aside things that he wanted me to put in the hands of our family back in Wisconsin and Illinois. I have boxed them up and will ship them off to Uncle Frank and Uncle Pete.

He was mostly lucid but every once in a while he would shout out, "You remember your Aunt Ginny, don't you?" He would pick-up her picture and wave it in my face before he clutched it to his heart. He was a dear old fellow. It always comforted him when I assured him that I did indeed remember her. However, I can't recall if he ever brought Aunt Ginny over to the States.

Sometimes he would start rambling about the old days and I admit he had me going at times.

One curious side note is that Uncle Al bequeathed directly to me a rather thick and shabby manuscript. He told me that only I was to handle it because it was his memoir of about his time with John Lennon and the Beatles. He stated that he had been 'poking at it' for many years off and on, but he hadn't given it the finishing touches he had planned to because the death of John and George Harrison had made the task too unpleasant to complete. I have started thumbing through the work and it's unbelievable if any of it's true. To me it reads like a secret history of the famed Beatles and the Mersey Beat days of the 1960s.

I recall hearing my mother, God rest her soul, brag about how Uncle Al had hung out with Beatles before they were big and how he had been a lecturer of John Lennon's at the art college. However, I never knew anything about his deeper relationship with the Beatles. Read the manuscript when I send you a copy and you'll see why I was so blown away by it. After all he was your brother, and everybody in the family knew how he was a master of Midwestern cracker barrel style of humor…you know, pulling your leg with a serious expression on his face, and then some hardcore facts popping up to the surface out of all the myths, tall tales and Irish blarney.

I had never really cared all that much about the Beatles until I read this work. I guess I was born too late to really get into the British Invasion thing. By the time I entered high school in the early 1970s they were already ancient history. But Uncle Al's manuscript has ignited my interest in them and their early days in tumble-down Liverpool. I am proud that the old boy entrusted me with the work.

Do you suppose your brother meant for his memoirs to be published? We can talk about it when I get home.

On second thought, perhaps the work would be stirring up a hornets' nest. Uncle Al made some pretty wild assertions; ones that would have landed him in court if he had published this when he was alive. It was all a long time ago, and the Beatles and their story now belong to the ages whether they like it or not. This book, fanciful or otherwise, would only add to their myth.

Anyway, I have an old Irishman to bury. I'll be back in Chicago in about a week. I hope some of the clan can make it over here to Liverpool for the burial.

Your loving nephew,
Steve

Being a True account of My Life and Times with the Beatles by Professor Albert Moran

PART 1: UPSTARTS
CHAPTER ONE

When the American naval warship landed at the Albert Docks, Liverpool, England, it unloaded me into a city that immediately depressed and enchanted me at the same time. How very much like my native Chicago was this dreary and crumbling port city. The endless blocks of council houses, pubs, factories and decaying buildings put me in mind of the Near North Side where I grew up. However, whereas Chicago was constantly putting up a struggle to renew itself whenever it began to die, the city of Liverpool appeared to be accepting its death rattles and impending demise with a strange peace of mind.

I suppose I really had no call to be surprised at the similarities between Liverpool and Chicago, for I had had almost two months onboard ship to study my guidebooks, histories and novels about England. Even before I had embarked upon my voyage across the Atlantic I had been an avowed Anglophile who prided himself on the knowledge I possessed off all things British.

But, as I was soon to discover, Liverpool isn't very English. Indeed, looking back on it now I realize that none of my books ever really dwelled upon the port city on the Mersey River. Most of the books that came across the ocean buried at the bottom of my great sea chest focused upon London, an England far removed from the one I was entering in both time and space.

Other than a few bare facts about the city, such as how King John granted it a charter as far back as 1207, and that Nathaniel Hawthorne, the American novelist, had been an ambassador there, I wasn't able to find much information on the place that would be my home for at least the next two years of my life.

After eight weeks living on a ship, where I earned my passage along with some spending cash teaching college level courses in art to Naval personnel, even dank and gray Liverpool seemed most charming to my pilgrim eyes.

I had arrived in England to take up a two year visiting lecturer post at the Liverpool College of Art. I, Dr. Albert Moran, was to be an instructor in art history, lettering, and illustration.

My friends and family, particularly my parents, had unsuccessfully tried to talk me out of my 'Limey adventure', as they called it, thinking it was just another one of the 'Al phases' that would dry up soon enough. But I had been restless and rootless at home, and like Melville's Ishmael, I knew it was time to push on when I began to have the urge to knock off peoples' hats. Besides, after some college, a two year hitch in the Army, followed by some more college, a brief stint as grammar school teacher, and then an additional two years in a graduate program to earn my Master of Arts in Art, followed by yet another three and a half years to earn a Doctorate in Art History, I had been doing nothing important with my life but hanging out in Chicago. I had earned my keep by working part time as an instructor in Renaissance Painters at the Chicago City College night school and working as a substitute art teacher for a string of Catholic high schools on the Near North Side. I saved money by living at home with my parents and three of my blue collar brothers.

I told people I was just holding on until I sold one of my paintings and could afford to buy a cottage up in Wisconsin on Lake Geneva. I also told people that once I had my dream cottage I would be free to devote the rest of my life to the pursuit of my art. Peace and quiet, I was certain, would bring all of my latent abilities out into the open and I would become a master.

On occasion, I would brag about all the money I would earn and women I would love. As I waited for the dreams to materialize, I made a few extra bucks sketching the rural faces of the Midwestern tourists who flocked to the coffee shops and ale houses of Chicago's fashionably 'beat' Old Town in search of the growing American counter-culture. I knew all too well that I was doing nothing with my life, and I was beginning to be overwhelmed with the weariness and sameness of my existence.

I came across the teaching post at the Liverpool College of Art through an announcement tacked upon a bulletin board in the Art Department's main office at the City College. I immediately applied for the position, mailing out my professional vita, along with my college transcripts, copies of my various degrees, and three letters of reference from colleagues perhaps a bit eager to get me away from Chicago. I also sent along several samples of my work: water colors, sketches, pencil and chalk works, and the likes.

I really never expected to be selected for the position, as I fully expected the competition to be stiff for a chance to work in Merry Ole England.

I was more than a little bit surprised, as well as frightened, when I was hired. Sure it is always a gratifying feeling to be chosen for a position over the other contestants, yet in the depths of my heart I doubted if I truly wanted to be away from Chicago for two years. A two week jaunt across to Great Britain would be a dream come true, but a two year stay could be a nightmare. Looking back now I realize how parochial I was in my way of thinking. I felt safe on the Near North Side of Chicago, sleeping beneath my parents' roof. I loved the comfortable little room where I had grown up in. I lived and died for the Cubs and the Bears. I enjoyed going to the games with my brothers who were also my best friends in the world. I worshipped Mayor Richard Daley, the longtime ruler of my hometown. I knew all the shops, diners and restaurants along Addison Street and Clark Street. I took a great delight in singing Irish folk songs with the other drunks on Saturday nights at O'Leary's, Finn McCool's and the Ginger Man. The workingmen, police officers and newsboys were my pals. But most of all, I didn't have the heart to leave Chicago's Old Town, with its Wells and North Street Dives where I bartered colors for drinks, drawing pictures to have the loot so I could hear jazz, blues or the new sound called rock and roll. I had become a character in my own right in that strange Bohemian world recently made popular by Jack Kerouac's curious novel *On the Road.* Mostly, I was happy.

When the letter offering me a position arrived in the mail I acted sophisticated and mature, full of talk about all of the cultural benefits I would rake in from my time in Liverpool. I was full of broad hints of continental weekends as well. Deep down inside I knew I would miss Chicago.

Professor Griffith, my contact at the Art College, was at Albert Docks to greet me and to escort me to his home where I was to stay for a few days until I found an apartment of my own.

Teddy Griffith turned out to be a delightful and friendly man; one that many Americans nurtured on old movies about England would have easily stereotyped as the typical Mr. Chips: at once scholarly, eccentric and kindly. Teddy's wife also turned out to be, at least to my eyes, a caricature of the gentle and genteel English woman.

"Our Albert will be taking digs just a stone's throw away from the College. All the arrangements have been made," Teddy announced to Mrs. Griffith and I one night at supper.

"Oh, dear, I do hope you've found a place fitting for an instructor at the College," fretted Mrs. Griffith.

"Come now, my dear, this isn't Oxford or Cambridge."

"As long as it's cheap and quiet I don't much care, really," I said casually, though inward I was excited. I thought Teddy would never get around to finding me a place of my own. The Griffiths were neat people but I wanted to strike out on my own. Besides, I hated the feeling of being underfoot all of the time.

"Cheap it is, my dear fellow. As for the quiet that all depends upon your definition of the word," Teddy said cheerfully. "It also depends on how loud the music is playing."

"What about music?" I asked dumbly.

"What are you on about, Teddy?" barked the wife.

"Rooms are cheap as all hell, near the College in the 8."

"Teddy, no!" protested Mrs. Griffith, grabbing her husband by the arm. "Albert, you simply must refuse to accept it. My husband's gone stark raving mad. He's found you a simply dreadful place in our city's horrid 8."

"Dear, don't scold me so, for I'm sure Al will love it," chuckled Teddy, hugging his wife.

"Is this 8 a red light district or something?" I asked.

"There may be a red light or two there, I rather think, but it isn't like your American combat zones or anything that exotic. After all, Liverpool is still England and not Hong Kong. Rather, the 8 is the part of Liverpool where all of the area's poets, painters, musicians, angry young men, rebels and beatniks hang out. Your Jack Kerouac would feel right at home there, as would any self-respecting American beatnik, although I'm afraid it is rather a letdown in comparison to Greenwich Village."

"Beatniks in England," I reflected. "I never expected to see any of those outside of the Village or North Beach or Old Town, where I come from."

"We'll have a look see after supper."

"Teddy?" asked Mrs. Griffith. "Did this Jack Kerouac ever teach at the Art College?"

CHAPTER TWO

It was a lovely August evening with a fair breeze coming in from over the Irish Sea. The streets of Liverpool were crowded with people, mostly young ones, enjoying the last balmy evenings of the summer.

My digs were small enough: a dank bedroom, a small living room, an even smaller dining room (which I intended to use as my studio) and a wee kitchen with a minuscule window that looked out upon the Roman Catholic Metropolitan Cathedral of Christ the King and the Anglican Church of Christ over on Hope Street.

The landlady was a blond, blowsy and busty woman in her late thirties who also happened to be a widow like so many landladies in English fiction. Mrs. Lampkins may have even learned her trade from Mrs. Hudson, the prototypical landlady from the Sherlock Holmes stories. She willingly agreed to tidy up my rooms and do my laundry for a few extra quid a week, adding that she would throw in a cup of tea and friendly advice for free.

"I'd say I don't fancy your job much, Dr. Moran. The Liverpool Art College, I mean. A right load of scruffy long hairs, if you ask me. And their lady friends aren't much better. Mind you don't mix with the likes of them. Have you in court for child support if given a chance if you so much as wink at 'em, and you such a nice American scholar and all. They're failures, one and all, if you ask me. If only you could find a post at Oxford or Cambridge than you'd see the finest of England's youth. Such fine schools, indeed: the pride of the British Isles, they are. I'm sure a gentleman of your education and background could easily get a position at one or the other. Let me call me cousin Alfie. He's a janitor down at Oxford although he's so much more than that, and he knows people, he does."

"Mrs. Lampkins, I think this position in Liverpool will suit me just fine," I was finally able to blurt out.

"Oh well, if it pleases you, sir," she said doubtfully, refilling my cup of tea. "But don't be too satisfied with it. Oxford or Cambridge would be the places to be, sir."

"I'm sure Dr. Moran will be happy here in our city," put in Teddy, giving me a sly wink.

When it was time to leave Mrs. Lampkins gripped my hand and led me out the door with a sheepish grin across her face."

"Nice lady," I remarked when we were back in the streets.

"Wot's that then mate?"

"Huh?"

"I'm just using some scouse on you, auld son. This is Liverpool and the Liverpudlians don't speak English, they speak ancient scouse, a weird sort of dialect spoken only in these parts. My friends in the field of linguistics assure me that scouse is a variation of the Irish brogue and Shakespearean English with a large pinch of countryside Welsh thrown in."

"What does scouse mean?"

"It originally referred to a sort of Irish stew the people of the city used to slap together to eat in the last century when times were hard. You know, like a Mulligan stew with a little off this and a little bit of that thrown into it."

"It sounds very interesting."

"I say, do you fancy C and W, old man?"

"Are you talking more of the local lingo to me?"

"C and W is what we call your American country and western music in Liverpool. You should know the sound."

"Mostly country music comes from the south or the west. Me, I'm from the far north. In Chicago C and W is considered low brow music listened to by hicks and hillbillies. However, my dad likes it a bit."

"Then Liverpool is full of these hicks and hillbillies, for

we're right batty for the sound."

"I get the picture."

"Slim Whitman, do you know him? He's playing at the Philharmonic tonight. He's quite good. Shall we take a look?"

"Sounds good," I lied, vaguely remembering Slim as a yodeling cowboy with greasy hair and glittering clothes.

"Then we're off," shouted Teddy, apparently a big fan of the rhinestone cowboy.

I tried to act pleased but I wasn't homesick enough to be in the mood for country music. I thought back to the old George Gogol radio program on Saturday night that featured the very worst of campy C and W. Then I thought about how in recent years my father was a big fan of the Barn Dance television show that was on every Saturday night just before Jackie Gleason. I couldn't see how people in England could be remotely interested in moonshine music from Mississippi.

Nonetheless, the Philharmonic turned out to be a good choice, for the hall was packed with young men and women. It gave me a chance to get my bearings on the social scene, as well as the opportunity to look over the women.

I was almost floored at the long and sustained greeting Slim Whitman received from the audience, both male and female. I rather thought this side burned cowboy with his boots, gawdy clothes, slicked back hair and flexing voice was rather vulgar and third rate.

"I don't get it, Teddy," I said after the third or fourth number. "What's all the fuss about? Hell, this guy couldn't even play in the Grand Ole Opry in Nashville on an off night."

"You don't say," Teddy answered with wide-eyed surprise. I had the feeling I had hurt his pride by my remark. "Slim is quite the rage these days. The only person who rivals him is Ernest Tubbs, another Yank who'll be playing here next month. We simply must take Mr. Tubbs in. Also Al, do keep your opinions about Slim to yourself. Remember, this is Liverpool, where we're starved for things that come from your side of the pond."

Three young women wandered by in the aisle and they greeted Teddy with great fanfare.

"Mr. Griffith!"

"Hello, ladies."

"Mr. Griffith, we didn't know you fancied Slim."

"Isn't Slim Whitman gear?"

"We're so surprised to see you here, sir."

"Are we behaving ourselves like proper English ladies, Mr. Griffith?"

"Don't say English, for it stabs me poor Welsh heart."

Before Slim Whitman had the chance to rip off another crescendo that would bring the house down and the audience to its feet, Teddy introduced me.

Albert, please meet Cynthia Powell, Ginny Browne and Mary Tag," introduced Teddy. "Ladies, Dr. Moran here will be one of your instructors at the Art College this year."

The three women greeted me in a shy and demure fashion.

"Pleased to meet you, ladies," I said.

"You're a Yank!" they almost shouted as one in perfect harmony.

"Americans are very much 'in', old man," explained Teddy, patting me on the back. "Enjoy it while it lasts."

"Where are you from?" asked the one named Ginny Browne who happened to be the cutest."

"Chicago."

"Home of the blues," she said knowingly.

"Do you swing to R and B, sir?" asked Mary Tag, a tall, gangling thing.

"Is that something like C and W?" I said dumbly.

"Rhythm and Blues," Teddy clued me in, adding, "its' almost as big as C and W in this city."

"Oh sure, I dig R and B."

"Are you wild for R and B?" asked Ginny Browne.

"Sure thing," I lied. I only liked the sound in a mild way but I kept that to myself because I didn't want to lose my audience. I actually preferred jazz and said as much. "Jazz is another form of Negro music. I love it."

"All that horn tooting business doesn't go well with us Scousers," Ginny said with a curl of contempt on her lips.

"Do you like Rock n Roll?" I asked in hopes of regaining her good graces. I wondered if the Brits called it R and R.

"It is gear!" she roared.

"Yes, it's becoming very popular in America," I put in. Like R and B, I only had a mild interest in the current Rock and Roll scene. Actually my brothers Pete and Frank were bigger fans than I was.

"Did you bring along any records with you?" asked Ginny, who impressed me with her shapely body, pretty brunette hair, and the impish smile that played across her sassy face. To me the girl was sexy, even if her white socks were drooping. While the other two were reserved, this girl seemed to be very bold. She also appeared to know her music very well.

"Yes, I bought along some to keep me from being homesick."

"Do you have any Little Richard?"

"I have one or two of his records. My brother Pete dragged me off to one of his concerts. I think he's more energetic than Elvis. He's certainly more powerful than a lot of those sappy white guys like Pat Boone and Perry Como."

Mr. Whitman sang a few more songs.

Ginny turned around in her seat to ask, "Which records do you have of Little Richard's?"

"Let's see: *Long Tall Sally*; *Jenny, Jenny*; *Lucille*; and some others. He's pretty keen but he's no threat to Beethoven."

"Ah, roll over Beethoven," Ginny jested to the amusement of the others.

"There's no respect for the masters of the classical music in Liverpool," noted Teddy.

"Do you like Buddy Holly?" asked Mary Tag, ignoring Teddy's remark.

"Yeah, he's cool. My brother Frank cried when Buddy died in that plane crash in Iowa."

"Many people cried in Liverpool as well, like me bloke," put in the one named Cynthia, who was also a pretty lass.

"Do you have any Fats Domino?" cut in Ginny.

"You should all come and look for yourself."

"Is that official like, Dr. Moran? No fooling'? It'll be dodgy if we show up unexpected like to take up your offer."

"Yeah, it's official."

"It won't be cheeky of me showing up on your doorsteps and asking for a peek at your labels?"

I realized she was now speaking for my ears only, her voice being low, soft and teasing.

"Please come by. It's only a short walk from here," I said, relieved Teddy was involved in a conversation with the other two.

"Why don't you show me the records now, darling? Come on, then, let's have a look now. Wot da you say, huh?"

"But," I slurred, "what about the show here?"

"Don't act so knackered, there'll be other shows."

Without so much as a 'goodbye' to the others, Ginny

dragged me out of the music hall. Many young teenagers in black leather jackets were loitering around outside. The miniature James Deans snorted when they saw the pretty coed dragging along an older man who was at least twice her age.

"Steady now, guv," called out one of the toughs as the others laughed on.

"Gin, give the poor auld bloke a running start, eh?"

"Now daughter be gentle with me da, will you?"

"Hey granddad, ye sure ye still got the stuff?"

"Got the spunk, old punk?"

They were only teasing, so I snarled back in my smartass street voice, "time to go home to bed kiddies."

They exchanged surprised glances as if my accent had thrown them off course for a moment.

"No hard feelings, then, Yank," called out the one who had started it all.

"No hard feelings, men!" I called back into the night as I was being pulled along by Ginny who had been aloof throughout the heckling.

"They're only having one on you; taking the piss out of you, as it's called here. No need to tarry over their likes. Please think of your status. Don't flip out over a slagging."

"I am only dishing it right back to them. Besides, what's the hurry? My records aren't going anywhere."

"But I am, luv. The night is short and I can't be larking about when there are so many places to go and people to see."

"You're more popular than the Queen," I teased.

"Quite so!"

The conversation died as we reached a set of street lights. Several large trucks rumbled past.

"We call them lorries over here, not trucks," observed

Ginny. "And they run on petrol, not gasoline."

"You know much about America. Have you visited it?"

"I have never left Liverpool, but two of my uncles are Cunard Yanks."

"Where do these Cunard guys come from?"

"You're like a lost child in the woods when it comes to our native tongue, aren't you?" she said with a delightful laugh that I had already begun to relish.

"Help me out of the woods, auntie."

"A Cunard Yank is a Liverpool sailor who has been to America several times on English ships from the Cunard line. Sometimes they even spend some time in your country, usually somewhere on the eastern seaboard. Me Uncle Bobby, me Mum's wee brother, has been to Boston, Philadelphia and New York. He likes New York the best. Do you like it?"

"Chicago is better."

"No, that isn't fair because it's your home. Besides, I don't know anything about it. Is it very big?"

"Chicago is our second biggest city."

"Hey, Liverpool is the second largest village in the U.K., leastways England. Is Chicago bigger than Liverpool?"

"I believe so," I answered. "But actually I like the smaller towns in Wisconsin better because they're very beautiful. They're only a few hours north of Chicago."

"Don't you mean duller?"

Before I could respond she cut me off by pulling up in front of a rather rundown pub with a tattered old sign that read *Ye Old Crackle* swinging above the entrance.

"Fancy buying me a pint, professor? If you're hard up, I can stand you a few."

"I have money," I almost snapped her head off. "I'm wondering if you're old enough to go inside of a pub."

Ginny laughed and tugged me into the place, hailing the bartender with a hearty greeting as she steered us over to empty seats at the bar. The joint was smoky but homey, the epitome of an English pub. From the looks of the clientele I surmised that the *Ye Old Crackle* catered to students from the Art College. The place had more than its share of turtleneck sweaters and beards. Ginny, who appeared to be well-known, greeted more than a few people, mostly men, in that hail and hearty fashion of hers.

"Black and Tan okay with you?" she asked, waving down a bartender.

"I'll take a beer."

"What do you think I'm on about here, then? A Black and Tan is bloody beer. Yank, you see, it's a drink that is half stout and half lager. But then I suppose you don't drink Guinness Stout in America."

"It's Irish beer, isn't it?"

"There you go, luv...I mean professor. Maybe it's from Dublin and that is indeed an Irish place, although I'm rotty at me geography."

"Yeah, Dublin is in Ireland. See, I'm already teaching you things."

"Squire Clancy, two pints of the Black and Tan. It's the Yank's first pull of the stout."

"Nah, I've had it before on St. Patrick's Day."

"So you celebrate that day, do you? Will ye be of Irish blood yourself, Dr. Moran?"

"Most of the people in Liverpool have Irish blood. We belong in the Republic rather than in the United Kingdom"

"Are you Irish?"

"I'm completely English, but the family bloodline is from Ireland. Being Irish in England isn't anything all that unusual."

"Do you know what the capital of Ireland is, Yank?"

Squire Clancy asked in a friendly manner.

"Dublin."

"Wrong you are, begging your pardon. It'll not be your Dublin fair city where the girls are so pretty. It's ratty Liverpool, it is. There's more bleeding Irish here than anywhere in Ireland, including Dublin."

The pints arrived.

"First one is on Squire Clancy, Yank! God bless you!" announced the bartender.

I toasted the bartender and took a gulp. It was strong but I liked it instantly. The sharp taste ringing inside of my mouth assured me I was finally in England. Black and Tans became my biggest addiction from that point on. Ginny was rapidly becoming my second addiction.

"Let's have another go at it, shall we luv?" asked Ginny, squeezing my arm when our drinks were drained.

The rounds came and went. The place became noisier and smokier as the evening progressed. Somewhere along the way a young man wearing a black leather jacket and horn-rimmed glasses pulled out an acoustic guitar and began to sing *My Bonnie* on top of a tiny stage. My brother Pete, a mere novice himself, could play better than that bespectacled youth after only three lessons. The voice was something else: a powerful, rugged voice with a raw scratch to it that somehow sliced through every word and sewed it up again into one piece of fine silk.

"Who's this guy?" I asked Ginny. "He's kind of good."

"You mean Johnny?" she responded. "Don't tell him he's good because the swine already thinks he's a cross between Buddy Holly and Jesus Christ. Cheeky bastard he is, alright."

"The glasses explain Buddy, but Jesus Christ too?"

"He's a terrible lad, that one...but really he's a sweetie pie all the same. Be wary of him, Dr. Moran, he's one of your students at the Arty and he eats instructors up with his morning kippers…that's if he shows up for classes."

For the better part of an hour this Johnny terror sang a sequence of songs ranging from Irish folk to American pop, from English dancehall to Negro R and B. There were also a few songs that I guess he had composed himself. I thought the lad had the most interest in Rock n Roll, for that's when his numbers rippled with energy.

In between sets I slurred into Ginny's ear: "Shall I buy this guy a brew?"

"He calls lager a bloody brew! Ha! How Yankee! Yes, please do, but you may not be able to shake him after, for he's a right sponge."

I ordered a pint of lager for this Johnny and left it on the table beside the stage as he performed *Good Golly Miss Molly*. He never blinked an eyelash though he had seen me.

"Pretty cocky," I declared as I retook my seat.

"He'll warm up to you soon enough, seeing that you're a friendly sort of chap. All you Yanks are friendly, aren't you?"

"Let me buy another round, Miss Browne."

"At school you can call me 'Miss Browne', but in a pub you can call me anything you wish as long as you're buying, but I like being called Gin or Ginny. You must think me an awful bird pulling you here like this and getting you to treat."

"I don't much care, Gin, but I'm wondering what the big shots at the Art College would say if they heard I had been drinking with one of my cuter female students. Things like this don't further one's career. And call me Al when we're not at the college."

"Don't be so square, Al. Nobody at the Arty cares about your social life."

Right when I was at the point of saying I had had my fill Johnny, the singer slapped me on the back, shouting "Thanks for the dram, mate."

"You're welcome, man. I like your stuff."

"It ain't me stuff, granddad. If you knew your pop you'd recognize Elvis, Buddy and Little Richard. I haven't written anything that smashing...yet."

"I like the kick you put into it."

"Are you a Yank?"

"I am an American."

"Must be just off the bloody ship, so you're a music fucking critic or what?"

"Guess again John, luv. He's a new professor at the Arty," cut in Gin.

"Wot's that, then? Are ye having me on then Gin, darling? A fucking professor in the flesh! That is just crazy, daddio!"

"He's Dr. Al Moran from Chicago."

"Mr. Al Capone from Chicago," snorted this Johnny. I wasn't sure I liked the boy or not. Surely he was fascinating, this cross between Buddy and Jesus...or was he a cross between Elvis and Andy Capp? But he was a very formidable young man with a forbidding air about him. He appeared to be ready to jump down my throat at the slightest provocation. For his part perhaps he was intrigued by me while feigning a bored air.

"My name is Dr. Al Moran, not Mr. Al Capone."

"Sounds like the name of a bloody gangster to me. All you Yanks are probably in the Mafia."

"My great uncle was Bugs Moran, who was Capone's biggest rival during prohibition," I joked, connecting my name to that of another one of Chicago's famous beer barons in the 1920s.

"Bugs Bunny, you say? Now you're a rabbit. Do you like your carrots cooked or raw, doc?"

"I like them far away from drunk assholes who can't play the guitar for shit."

"Wot's that, then?"

"Oh John, have done with it and be civil for crying out loud. And after this gent stood you a round and him only arrived in town. It's a long shot more than you'll ever do for him, John Lennon."

"There's where you're wrong Gin, me heart. I'm sure the Yank will benefit in the long run when I make me way to the toppermost of the poppermost. He'll find me right pleasant when I'm on the top."

The shouting made me lose my way during this fast Liverpudlian repartee. I sulked into silence before offering a rather nasty, "So you see yourself as a big shot singer Johnny?"

"Mister to you!"

"Mr. Lemmon," I snapped back. "You're a fucking piece of Limey fruit."

Gin burst out laughing at my remark but this Lennon only glared a moment before slamming down his empty glass and stamping back to his chair on the stage. I decide in favor of a quick truce so I talked Gin into carrying over another pint to Lennon. Without a word he grabbed the pint and chugged it in one gulp.

"He's not too mad," Gin whispered to me when she sat down again.

"Before I start me next set," John growled into the mike, "And before Mr. Al Bugs Moran Dr. Capone Bunny gets a knee trembler from Missy Ginny Brownie Browne Bunny, his wife, I'd like for the yank to come up here and give us a song from the land of Frito Corn Chips, or is that the Land of the Free…bumblebee…b…buttocks? Oh well, come on up Al Moran."

What it all meant was over my whirling head except that several arms steered me up to the stage.

"Have a bit of a sing song for our pleasure Al," John said

neatly.

"Hooray for the Yank!" Clancy the bartender shouted.

"Swing, professor, swing," encouraged Gin somewhere out there among the staring faces.

My mind flickered blank until I remembered the Woody Guthrie number, *This Land is Your Land*, a tune I had heard many times by the folkies in Old Towne. I was afraid I'd forget the words, but I was profoundly relieved when John as well as the audience sang along. Apparently the audience was familiar with the song. When the song concluded I was dismissed from the tiny stage with a curt nod of John's head.

"Do you like that Lennon?" I asked Gin as we walked towards my tiny apartment. Having noticed my drunken condition she had offered to walk me home. I used my drunkenness as an excuse to lean against her.

"He's a loveable swine, that's what all of us girls at the Arty say about him. Mind you, many people detest him. He can be a right bully when he has a mind to. But really, he'll grow on you, given time."

"But don't warts grow on you too," I cracked.

"Wot's all this, then?"

"Toppermost of the poppermost! He talked strangely. I don't know much about his artwork but he does have a poetic ring to him."

"I think he does a bit of writing as well."

"He never said anything about his drawing."

"Maybe you won't fancy his stuff. It gives one an ill feeling. You'll see for yourself soon enough. As for being an artist maybe he's not much of one with brushes, oils, paints and such. But I reckon he's an artist right enough when it comes to music. Did you dig his Buddy specks?"

"John Lennon wears 'Buddy specks'! Ha! I thought as much. At least he has the right look."

"Johnny hates glasses but he'll wear them if Buddy is on his mind and he needs some encouragement to rock."

"What's a knee trembler?"

She began to lose herself in laughter. I started to laugh myself when I saw the tears streaming down her face.

"That terrible, terrible boy," she gasped in between burst of laughter, "saying such a naughty thing in front of all those people."

"Well, what is a knee trembler?" I persisted, anticipating the worst.

"I'll show you if you promise not to tell a soul," she said coyly, her voice suddenly taking on a wicked tone.

"Okay, I promise."

Once again this young English woman took me by the hand and took charge of things, this time guiding me into a dark and deserted alley. My mind began to clear somewhat when she reached for my belt.

"Up against the wall, gently then," she instructed.

"Like this?" I pondered; my attempt clumsy and drunken.

"Are your knees trembling yet, luv?" she asked after a short while.

"Why yes, they are…wow!"

As the two of us pressed against the wall one could almost imagine the old brick itself flaking into thousands of tiny bits and pieces. Now having learned what a knee trembler was, I would soon learn that the flaking of the building was called Liverpool dandruff.

"We never had a chance to listen to your records, luv," cooed Gin.

"We'll make it another time."

CHAPTER THREE

I can't say that having sexual intercourse with a student is a very good idea no matter how lovely and willing she happens to be. And the memory of my first English knee trembler had left me delighted as well as horrified as I entered the Liverpool College of Art to begin my first day as an art instructor.

The college was a tumbled down old place made up of grime stone and sickly coated plaster, something deserving of destruction by Hitler's air war. The place reminded me of the battered high schools in the Negro section of the South Side of Chicago. I had the feeling I was starring in a seedy black and white 1930s British movie, one where most Americans couldn't understand the accent and thought it too boring. I only hoped I was going to be the good guy in the script.

My first class began at nine so I timed it where I would walk into the room at just about nine too. It was my intention to keep the students waiting in a bit of suspense, wondering who their art history professor would be. I had also learned from previous experience that it was almost a universal tradition that students be allowed to show up late for the first day of class, so I wanted to be a tad late to allow the slowpokes a few extra minutes to get in their seats to save me the annoyance of looking at people strolling in after the bell had rung.

Gulping a final sip of water at the fountain I realized I was stalling because I was nervous and trying to avoid that first plunge into the water. Putting on my best Joe Cool look, my stomach nearly to the bursting point with butterflies, I stepped into the classroom.

"Just let them get used to you, Al, lad, on the first day," Teddy had advised me. "Give them a chance to have a looksee. I wager they'll warm up to you soon enough."

I felt the sensations that Glenn Ford must have had when he stepped into the classroom full of black leathered rowdy students in the movie, *A Black Board Jungle*. People who have never taught before can't understand the anxiety all teachers experience on the first day of class. I almost expected an eraser to be tossed at my head. Instead I was greeted by the essentially friendly, if curious faces of roughly thirty students. I began to feel somewhat better knowing my students weren't New York punks.

"Good morning class. I'm Dr. Moran and I will be your lecturer in Art History for this term. Oh, by the way, if you think I'm talking funny it's not because I'm from Birmingham," I cracked, trying hard not to notice Gin, who was trying to go unnoticed in the back of the classroom.

There was delighted laughter.

"And I'm not a Cockney from London, either."

More laughter filled the lecture hall.

"I'm an American from Chicago who will be teaching here at your college for the next two years."

Their curiosity appeared to grow as did their smiles. I knew I was off to a good start as I picked up the class roster and began to take roll.

"Anderson."

"Here I am, sir."

"Browne."

"Right over here, Dr. Moran."

It was a relief to not hear her say, "Over here, luv."

"Carricker."

"Aye."

"Furlong."

"Present, sir."

"Lennon."

There was no response from the class.

"Mr. John Lennon," I repeated.

There was still no answer.

"Mr. Lennon isn't here on the first day of classes?" I asked, frowning down at the name on the roster.

"Begging your pardon, Dr. Moran," called a pretty blonde who I recognized as Cynthia Powell, one of the girls I had met with Gin at the Slim Whitman concert.

"What is it, miss?"

"Johnny, I mean Mr. Lennon will probably not be here today. He's sick. Headache, I should think. Sorry, sir."

Several snickers greeted Cynthia's remark.

"Sir, he probably won't be here all week," added a dark handsome fellow.

"Or all term, for that matter," tossed in Gin.

"So Mr. Lennon is somewhat of a slacker?" I asked with good humor. "Ah yes, I think I've heard of him before." I pretended to think, wondering if I should mention that I heard him singing in a pub.

"Maybe you have smelled the rotter, sir," one woman said sharply. "He smells like fish n chips, that one does."

"Hangs all over him, that."

"It does not, you terrible liars," cried out Cynthia, turning red in the face. So this was Lennon's girlfriend!

"Sorry, Cynth, we all know you love our John," said a very goofy looking lad, bringing on more high jinks from the others and a hard glare from Cynthia.

"Well, our John may be a slacker, but he can sure rock n roll," I said.

By the mentioning of the expression 'rock n roll' I had managed to win back the attention of my audience.

"Mohammed," I started on the roll again.

"Aye, aye, Captain Moran," called out the dark lad.

"Mason."

"Here."

"Powell."

"Yes, sir, I'm here."

After roll it seemed I had just enough time to make some desultory remarks on the early history of art and to give a brief outline of the course structure.

"Class dismissed."

As I walk down the hallway to my next class I was joined by Geoff Mohammed, the dark looking chap who I took to be an Arab, Tony Carricker and Gerry Marsden. Their burning good nature and genuine interest in me made me relax. For the first time I was delighted to actually be a teacher in England.

"I say, Dr. Moran, do you dig rock n roll?" asked Geoff.

"I love it."

Since being in Liverpool I realized the tremendous influence American music had upon the youth of Britain and I intended to use that interest to my advantage.

"Who's your favorite?" asked Tony.

"Elvis, of course; he's the King," I responded, echoing a thousand headlines.

"Maybe that," said the one named Marsden, only partially agreeing with me. "But look out Elvis, Buddy Holly almost closed in on yer. Buddy would have won by now 'cepting he got hisself killed and all."

"Go on now, Gerry, you're being daft."

"Am I, then?"

"What's your favorite spin, Dr. Moran?"

"Sorry."

"Disc," he answered.

"Record, like," explained Marsden.

I reached for a title and replied "Jailhouse Rock."

My answer apparently satisfied my new mates. We all would have liked to have carried on the conversation but the next class was to begin.

I recognized several of my students from the earlier class, including Gin and Cynthia. I did basically the same introduction as before only modifying it to acknowledge my previous class and exchanging my stray remarks about art history for the ones about illustration. Once again Lennon was listed on the roster but absent from class.

Halfway through the period a terrible din suddenly rang out in the hallway, sounding like a sea chantey by a drunken sailor painting the town red on his shore leave.

The voice sang:

"Sugar in the morning

Sugar in the evening

Sugar at suppertime."

Several of the students looked aghast. Cynthia blushed noticeably and literally buried her head in the notebook. Tony and Geoff exchanged soft chuckles. Marsden winked at me and smiled apologetically. I caught the eye of Gin who soundlessly mouthed the name, "Lennon."

On the silent 'N', as if following a script and answering a cue, John Lennon, the arty bad boy stepped into the room in what smelled like the clothes he had been wearing on the previous Saturday night. His aroma indeed was that of fish n chips, along with the mixed fragrances of beer, sweat and the past of Liverpool. It immediately assaulted and insulted the noses of everybody present with the possible exception of Cynthia.

"Bless me soul if it isn't Mr. Al Capone from Chicago."

The uneasy quiet that prevailed indicated that everybody was waiting to see how the first meeting between Dr. Moran, lecturer and Mr. Lennon, student would unfold. It was to be a pivotal moment for my future at the college. I was standing judgment more than John.

"I am pleased to see you again, Mr. Long John Silver. Ah, but that's only on Saturdays when we're off duty, but for the rest of the week you're Mr. Lennon the serious student and I'm Dr. Moran your serious lecturer. Please join the rest of the class and please listen with attention to my lecture the way I listened to you when you sang in the club. That's Jake, I think."

My off-the-cuff gibberish was ample enough to quell any immediate trouble, for John quietly took his seat and whispered to Cynthia. For her part, Miss Powell ignored him in the point-blank fashion, her pen scribbling away as I spoke.

At the end of the period Marsden yelled out to me in a cheerful manner, "If you fancy an earful of home grown Yank music have a listen to Radio Luxembourg."

I jotted the name down in a notebook.

"It's the radio station for your fighting lads stationed over in Germany," explained Geoff.

Then I called Lennon aside. Ground rules had to be set up.

"Lennon, your presence has an electrifying effect."

"Does it now, then?" he chortled, feigning boredom while it was quite plain to see he was tickled by my statement.

"It'd be great if we could have you in earlier so we could savor your energy a bit longer."

"Earlier it is, doc. Five minutes, certainly."

"Yes. Five minutes before class would give us a chance to chat. Yes. That's a good idea," I countered.

No, John Lennon never became a model student because of my words of flattery. In fact he missed my lettering class later that very afternoon and he missed all of my classes for the rest of the week. I had mixed feelings about it. He did have a certain sort of aura about him that made him exotic in some way. He was really a Dickensian rough cut who was also an enchanting character: pure English, smelling of fish n chips, the sea, the pubs, and the Merseyside itself. He was a mix of Oliver Twist, Andy Capp and Elvis. What's more, others felt his magic too. I soon learned he was the ringleader of the resident Beatniks at the college. Our Lennon was a rebel without a cause, a real Jack Kerouac creation gone John Bull, stimulating and challenging his more conservative classmates onwards.

On the other hand, this Lennon frightened me. Not in a physical sense so much as a spiritual one. I had at least forty pounds on the slender English youth, coupled with ten or fifteen Golden Gloves beneath my belt, not to mention more than a few North side gang rumbles, wrestling matches with my brothers, and grammar schoolyard scuffles. Nonetheless, I was leery of his sharp tongue and tormenting mind. I also suspected that if the two of us competed for the class's attention that he would win easily every time. Still I felt vaguely hurt whenever he didn't show up for my lectures. I have never been able to understand why John, like many others, believed that their refusal to receive an education would somehow change the world.

Lennon apart I had a shipload of other concerns to worry about. There were lesson plans to prepare, assignments to correct, and projects to design. There was also my ongoing adjustment to English ways. Liverpool was still being absorbed into my very soul. I also had to work at adapting my speech to be fully understood and, too, my ears still weren't completely dialed into the dips and hops of the scouse.

On a more embarrassing note: I had to learn to live with the sudden increase in my sex drive. What was it that made me incredibly lusty for just about every Liverpudlian in a skirt? The smiles, the lilting voices, the long skirts, the attempts to be just like Yankee ladies in the movies, and the Irish looks. All of it seemed to turn me on. The hearty salty sea air that waffled into the city from the Irish Sea may have tickled my nose with its magical wand, setting off a weird Freudian chain of reaction inside of me. Sad to say, my love life was barren.

Then one day at tea Mrs. Lampkins, my widowed landlady, boldly hinted that I could have more than the usual scones. I tallied up inside of my head that she was a good ten years my senior, but I decided to subtract a few years due to her efforts.

"Maybe you don't fancy me much, Dr. Moran. I am losing my looks. Going to pot and there's no need for me to deny it."

"You're lovely and you have a fine figure."

"So you've been looking, have ye, naughty boy?" she laughed as she stood up and spun around so I could have a better look at her well-framed if slightly heavy form.

"It's hard to avoid looking."

"You're a bold American!"

Her breasts were large and inviting. Her plump backside promised a safe landing. I was sold on the idea.

"And you with all those pretty Artsy pies at the College to tend you. Surely they bring a glitter to your eyes quicker than the likes of me."

"You're wrong there," I replied, reaching for what had been offered.

"The neighbors must not know, luv. This is Liverpool. People love to talk."

On the other hand, Gin Browne stayed far away from me in some weird sort of penance since our 'knee trembling' lesson. The more I saw her in my classes, the more I secretly wanted to kiss her again. I was hoping to lover her properly on our second encounter. However, I was making no progress.

Once in the hallway, carrying on the charade, she called out, "Good afternoon, Dr. Moran."

I wondered how a woman who had taken my *Jolly Roger*

into her hand and directed it into herself as we leaned against an old warehouse could call me Dr. Moran in such a formal fashion. I was hurt.

CHAPTER FOUR

One day when I was leaving the Art College I chanced to spot John Lennon shuffling down the street in his black leather jacket. He reminded me of Vic Morrow in *The Blackboard Jungle*: the punk with a chip on his shoulders. I was eager to have a few words with him concerning his checkerboard attendance in my classes, so I followed him.

Lennon stopped in front of the Liverpool Institute, the snooty vocational school next to the college, where he was joined by two other greasy-haired boys who were also wearing black leather coats. With Lennon in the middle the three moved on. It seemed John was doing all the directing as the three crossed over to Falkner Street and entered a chip shop. I slowed down my pace to give them a chance to settle in.

When I entered the small shop my nostrils were assaulted by the puffs of grilled air smoke. No wonder Lennon smelled like fish and chips. I could see three teenagers out of the corner of my eye. They were absorbed in talk but not deeply enough for John to overlook me. I was putting in my order when a voice called out: "Dr. Moran! Over here, sir!" It was Lennon's voice, all natural and respectful. I put my finger in the air to indicate I would be over in a moment after I received my order.

"Lennon, long time, no see," I saluted as I approached their table.

He looked slightly puffed when the others recognized my Americanized greeting.

"So sorry that, guv, but been tied up at home. Me auntie has taken sick like."

The two other boys tittered. One of the lads was tall and nicely made with dark bluish-black hair and a round cherub face that contained two dark eyes. His looks were striking, but I thought it strange how he had his coat to the very top in spite of the heat inside of the shop. When he noticed I was giving him the once over the smile left his face and he assumed a rather nervous, timid look like he wasn't sure how I, as a figure of authority, would react to John's sass.

The other chap was also on the tall side, but he was extremely gaunt. He may have been the thinnest Brit I had ever met to date. The lad almost bordered on being corpselike. His long hair and serious demeanor gave him an elfin appearance. When I spoke his lips curled over slightly in a half-mocking, half-respectful smirk.

"Well, I hope she gets better for we all miss you. The other kids are keen but they need a rocker to liven 'em up."

Lennon shrugged his shoulders but his companions were clearly impressed.

"Hon, mister, his aunt, that'll be Mrs. Mimi Stanley, has took ill like this past week, really, but the doctor, a Doctor Roberts, most respected in Woolton, has announced her fit most recently, so henceforth Johnny, er, Mr. Lennon will be able to attend school this Monday come."

It was such a mouthful from such a grave looking young fellow. I saw it as a lot of bullshit but vintage scouse too: all pulling your leg while they're being respectful. I suppose working class English behavior was a device invented centuries before by the defeated Saxon, who needed a means to insulate themselves against their Norman invaders while maintaining a sense of dignity.

"Are you two art students?" I asked.

"Ha, that," hooted Lennon. "If they'd unbutton their jackets you'd see their school shirts. That's why Paul here always closes all of his buttons; it's to hide his uniform. Art students, me arse!"

The gaunt one snorted, "I'd be lucky to earn one O level much less get into the Arty. That is, unless me auntie can use her influence and pounds to get me in like Johnny's auld one did."

"Have done with it, son," snapped John. "It was me

bleeding naturally given talent as an artist that battered the castle door in. Mr. Capone…er, yes sir… Moran, ran, run, running, will soon find out. Me abilities will shine if he allows me back into his class after me leave of absence."

"No problem Lennon, Lemon, Lenten, Lime," I jested in return.

"I'd like to go to the Arty myself, sir," the dark one said earnestly, tugging at my sleeves. "But the auld one, the gaffer, my pader, wants me to read literature at the University of London so I can teach school. He says teaching is the great one for being a job for life."

"He'd know about that, wouldn't he," cut in John, "him having been with the Cotton Exchange since the 14-18 war."

"What's a pader?"

"Mr. Jim McCartney, his dad," explained the gaunt one.

"Maybe in the future I could use you as a reference, sir. And maybe someday I can do you a good turn, like. Square it up, see. I have lovely drawings and the likes, then?"

"Stick to writing songs Paul, my son," crabbed John. "One bloody painter per group allowed."

"Do you mean gang?" I asked, unsure if gangs ruled and ruined the streets in Liverpool as they were doing in Chicago.

"I mean a group as in *band*. You know, with guitars and such," said the gaunt one, who seemed to be a likeable fellow in spite of his dourness.

"By the by, lads, this distinguished American gent is Professor Albert Moran, currently of the Liverpool Art College. However, prior to holding this post Dr. Moran was Mr. Al Capone, a notorious gangster back in Chicago."

The two boys laughed, though their reactions were slow from nervousness. It was obvious that John's disrespectful approach to adults still embarrassed them as much as it delighted them.

"Good to meet you guys," I announced, sticking out my hand.

"You have a lot to learn about Liverpool, Dr. Moran," said the dark one, offering me one of his fries. "Me name is Paul McCartney."

"Paulie, be nice, for the poor man has only just gotten off the boat, hasn't he," snapped John, putting this Paul in his proper place.

I was rather taken back by John's newly found attitude towards me, it was almost deferential. It began to dawn upon me that he was showing off for the benefit of his two mates, rubbing in the fact that he was an adult, an art student, able to talk on a natural man to man level with a professor, while they were still only high school boys. Somehow his talking with me gave John a higher status.

"Dr. Moran, I hope you like it here, and me name is Harrison," said this Harrison, firmly shaking my hand.

"Good to meet you, Mr. Harrison."

"Nah, that's me Da. My name is George."

"Okay, George Harrison."

"Well, I'm off to catch the bus. Me Da will be passing over directly," said George, standing up.

"What's the big hurry then, son?" asked John.

"Can't keep me Ma's supper waiting in the oven, now can I? The auld one would clobber me, like."

George smiled, waved and left.

"George's old gaffer drives a bus for the city of Liverpool. Now that's something a working class lad can boast about to his mates: you know, getting free rides on the bloody bus, and it being against the city rules and such."

"Nice guy," I said, making conversation.

"He's gear on guitar, he's our lead."

"You mean he's the leader of the group?"

"No, no, no, Mr. Al Capone Moran," snapped John, losing patience with me and my stupid questions. "I'm the leader, mate. Named the bloody group Long John and the Silver Beatles, didn't I, then?"

"Good name for a band," I lied.

"We like it right enough," John said testily.

"We used to be Johnny and the Moondogs," said the dark one. "Before that we were the Quarrymen in honor of Quarry Bank School, a rotty, scary dump of a prison, really. It being a really terrible place to borrow a name from, we decided to drop it. What's you saying to that, Johnny?"

"Hey, maybe Johnny and the Beatles sounds better more American than fucking Long John and the Silver Beatles. What do you say to that, what, Mr. Capone, er, Dr. Moran from Chicago."

"No, I prefer Long John and the Silver Beatles. It's more English sounding, and you are an English Band. But, without you biting my head off, what is a Silver Beatle?"

"It's something on the note of Buddy Holly and the Crickets. You know, Crickets, Beatles: an insect that rock and rolls like," explained the dark one.

"No, that's not it at all, son," cut in Lennon. "You have it all wrong, that. Beatles is derived from the word 'beat,' like heartbeat, drumbeat, rock n roll beat. That's why we spell it with an 'a' and not 'e'. It's all to do with the word 'beat'."

"Like the Beat generation from my country?" I suggested.

"Shag off your bloody American Beatniks."

"Well, I'm off as well," cut in the dark one. "Me dad will be expecting his supper when he gets home from the Cotton Exchange. I do the cooking and the little brother, Michael he's called, does most of the cleaning since our Mum passed on. You know, died, like."

John visibly flushed at the mention of the work 'mum'.

"Why go into that one again, mate? She's gone for good, like me own mum, Julia. Let it alone, can't you?"

"Sorry, John...just talking," apologized Paul.

"Hey, what's your name again?"

"Paul McCartney."

Paul McCartney left after giving me a friendly nod. The expression on his face seemed as though he were putting me away inside of a cabinet for later use.

I sat alone with John, painfully aware of the awkward silence that had descended upon us. I wanted to talk with him to discover what made him tick. I kept my tongue still because I didn't want this interesting hooligan to realize how nosey I was about him.

"So what does your father do for a living, Lennon?" I asked cautiously, figuring I was on safe ground.

"How the hell should I know, Yank!" Lennon fairly barked at me. "The dirty swine shoved off and abandoned me and Julia when I was a lad. Good riddance to him, I say. Last we heard he was washing pots and pans on a Cunnard ship headed for Mars or New York. Probably in Chicago now, and your lot can keep the git."

"Relax John. Don't snap my head off any more. I don't like it. Besides, I'm not one of your school chums."

"Wot's that, then?" he thundered threateningly, his face darkening.

Here was a young man accustomed to getting his own way and who used violence and force to keep it that way. I wasn't buying any of that.

"Back off, Jack!" I growled back, feeling angry in spite of myself. I unconsciously clinched my fists.

"You act like you'd fancy a punch up with me, mate!"

"I'm not running away from one, pal. It's not the American way to run away from bad mannered bullies like you."

"Why don't you go back to your own country where you belong with the rest of your blooming rich country men!"

"Rich! My father worked in a factory for fifty years and my mother taught fifth graders at a poor Catholic school. My parents both had quite humble but honest positions, I assure you. Besides, rich people don't teach at Liverpool Art College. You know that well enough."

Lennon's face suddenly drained of its red bloodiness and a kindly smile broke out of the frown and his expression became calm. When I returned the smile I could see his body relaxing. Then out of the blue he cheekily asked if I could spot him another coke.

"So you're a working class lad beneath the cap and gown façade?" he asked, sipping the coke I had bought him.

"We call it blue collar in America. I grew up in a blue collar neighborhood, but I don't consider myself a working man, at least not a laborer like my father. I went to the University to earn my degrees so I could move up the social ladder."

"So you're a social climber, then, Dr. Moran?"

"I never thought of it that way. I never believed that me working in a factory would improve the lot of the workers. I never fell in with the Marxist 'up the workers' thing. Get out of the working class was my motto. Besides, my parents, especially my father, wanted me to better myself."

"And did you better yourself?"

"Ask me when I retire," I quipped. "At any rate I'd rather be teaching betters like you about art than working nine to five on an assembly line like my brothers."

"How did you manage to pay for your university book learning if your gaffer was only a common day laborer?"

"It was tough but I managed."

"Some of the working class skins in Liddypool get government grants. My Aunt Mimi uses some of the money she inherited from me Uncle Harry to get me through. Then I received a grant myself because I'm almost an orphan."

"I went to school on the G.I. Bill."

"What now? Gee Eyes Billboards?"

"Ha. The G.I. Bill is money the U.S. government pays to put veterans, that is, soldiers, sailors and marines, through college after they complete their military service. G.I. stands for government issue."

"You don't look like a soldier."

"I guess I wasn't much of one."

"Didn't you kill Kooks in Korea during the 1st war?" he asked, leaning forward. I was more than a bit taken back by his tasteless question.

"I never killed anybody, John. I was a peace time soldier stationed over in West Germany."

"Duetchland?" John literally shouted.

"Yes, I was in Germany."

"We're your barracks in Hamburg by any chance?"

"I was further south in Stuttgart, on the Austrian side. Hamburg is a northern seaport. However, I did visit Hamburg one time on a weekend pass and I had a blast. It's rough and ready port city."

"Me and the lads are trying to get Allan Williams to book us some playing gigs over in Hamburg. It's all the rage, playing in Germany. The Krauts love rock n roll. Derry and the Seniors, Gerry and the Pacemakers and Rory Storm and the Hurricanes want a chance to go over there and make some dosh playing in the big nightclubs. The lads and meself are right keen on giving it a whirl ourselves. Hamburg beats bloody Liverpool. Nothing ever happens here in the Pool. Why would you leave Chicago for this rat infested hole in the wall?"

"I wanted to see it, and it was the only gig I had a hook on for the time being."

"Well said Al, Dr. Al. now I must be off to catch the number 71."

"What is the number 71?"

"Me bloody bus for Woolton."

"Remember, John, I'd love to see more of you in my classes."

"You missed your calling in life, Albert. You should have been a priest," he said not unkindly.

"Education is important," I began to say before cutting myself off as his face began to change colors again. But I did say, "Maybe you'll need your degree from the Art College just in case the gigs stop for the Beatles. You know, education is sort of self-protection for your old age. We call it covering your behind in Chicago."

"It's Long John and the Silver Beatles, not the Beatles. And there are no gigs to stop because we can't get any to start with outside of an odd church dance."

"Regardless, you know I'm right about the college degree. Please think about it, anyways."

"Good afternoon, governor."

I sat and watched the slumping figure of John Lennon hurrying out of the fish n chip shop and racing down the street to catch to the bus to Woolton. Then I thought about Mrs. Lampkins. I was lost in a fantasy when Lennon suddenly reappeared and stuck his head into the restaurant, saying, "If you're interested, be at the Jacanda Coffee House this Saturday at eight. Bring Gin Browne. She's in love with me but she'll settle for less. Chow how now Browne cow."

"Don't take it on the lam, Sam, or people won't give a damn," I countered.

CHAPTER FIVE

Friday afternoon was always an emotionally satisfying time for me as the week's classes were finally behind me. The class rolls put away and papers to be corrected were put aside to only be pulled out later on Sunday evening. Friday around five o'clock meant I had survived another week in Liverpool.

The autumn day was rather rainy, but the temperature had a nice mild edge to it that was warm and cheerful. I was happily contemplating a tall foaming pint of Guinness when I heard somebody calling from behind me, "Dr. Moran!"

With my eyebrows slightly raised behind my glasses, I turned around to see Ginny Browne awkwardly navigating her legs beneath her tight skirt in an effort to catch up to me.

"Ah, Miss Browne," I said, not sure if we were on a professional or a personal level."

"Johnny wanted me to remind you about the Silver Beatles gig at the Jac Coffee House tomorrow night. It will be smashing. The scene will be fun even if the lads are off tune."

"Will you be going?" I asked with too much apparent hope. "I'd hate to sit by myself."

Her school girl's face frowned its way into a look of suspicion.

"Now I may be there, or then again maybe I shall not. It's all the same to me, really. And I'm asking myself why you should care, Albert Moran."

"Sorry I asked."

"I asked, wot's it to you, mate? You sound like a bloke what got ideas of his own."

"A simple 'buzz off buster' would suffice to get rid of me."

At this she smiled and said, "Really Al, I do like you, but

let's just have fun. Okay by you?"

"Okay by me," I lied.

"It's a bit early for a drop, but the pubs will be opening soon and I wouldn't snap your head off if you suggested a quick pint."

"It sounds good."

"But I wonder if you'd mind if we stopped a bit further down the road a ways. Too many Arties around here and I don't want the birds to go ape shit over you. They think you're right smashing, they do."

"Who sees me as smashing? I don't believe it!" I hooted.

"Granted, you're no Elvis or James Dean. You're a bit too well-covered for that. Plump, rather, don't you agree? But the birds all think you're frightfully nice and sexy in a Yankee way."

"Well covered?"

"Pudgy in the middle," she said, poking my belly with her index finger. I wished she would go on touching me. She had something poor Mrs. Lampkins was missing. It was some sort of raw sex appeal that one only found to exist in foreign and exotic women, at least that's how I, a lonely American wanderer, felt.

"I could sure afford to drop a few pounds."

"We call it stones here."

"Fat is fat."

"You look like Peter Ustinov, the actor."

A young paperboy passed on the street harking *The Daily Worker*, the local socialist paper.

"Here lad, let us have one now, like a good boy," called Gin.

"Yes, lady," answered the boy, dishing out a paper.

"Be a dear, Al, and pay the wee feller so he can run on home to his mommy and supper."

I dug out a few shillings.

"Thanks sir," said the newsboy, running on his way.

"*The Daily Worker*," I read the flag. "I take it it's the local commie rag."

"You Yanks don't cotton to Marx much, eh?"

"Since the Red Scare nobody in America wants to be labeled a commie," I remarked. The McCarthy Era was only a few years behind and my country was still on a witch hunt for anybody even remotely connected with communism.

"Yes, *The Daily Worker* is for us laboring folk. It's all 'up the workers' and all that Tommy rot. 'Hooray for the peoples' revolution' and so on. But don't fret it Al, we English don't have much faith in any type of politics or religion."

"I hope you don't have much faith in communism, because it isn't likely there will ever be a major working class revolution since the Russians screwed up theirs."

"Don't be such a sourpuss of a capitalist, my dear Yank."

"I'm a realist," I replied coolly. "As long as the workers are left their beer, sex and television they'll continue to pop out babies for the factories and salt mines. Most people are destined to be laborers."

"You're a cynic, luv," she snapped with a playful pout, rifling through the paper. "Save your capitalistic speeches for somebody who cares. Me, I'm only after looking for info on the band scene. You see, *The Daily Worker* is the only paper in Liverpool that has any interest in what's happening for us young people. In fact, the paper is right keen on the local bands here and they're spreading the word over to Birmingham and Manchester."

"Do they ever write about Lennon's band?"

"Ha, that!"

"Let's see, aren't they known as Long John and the Silver Beatles?"

"All that fancy stuff doesn't fool any of us one bit. The simple Beatles they are, and the simple Beatles they shall remain. And it doesn't matter if you spell it with an 'a' or 'e'. John Lennon's pretentions are bigger than his talents."

"At least the Beatles is an easier name to remember."

"Anyways, the Beatles have never rated very many lines in *The Daily Worker*. Really they're all over Gerry Marsden's lads, the Pacemakers, Derry and the Seniors, and Rory Storm and the Hurricanes that get the print because they're the best of the lot."

"I don't know the music scene in this town...yet."

"Ah, but you know Gerry Marsden from the Arty. Ger is the daft one with the goofy smile."

"Ah, you mean the funny kid."

"He's funny alright, that one," she said knowingly. "But he's a good soul for all that, not like Lennon who's part angel and part demon."

"Is Gerry a close friend of yours?" I nosed around.

She ignored my prying question, shouting, "Listen to this Al: 'The Mersey sound is the voice of 80,000 crumbling households and 30,000 people on the dole.' Sounds like the Liddie, don't it now?"

"Tell me more about this Mersey Sound."

"Yeah, you know, the Mersey River, the Mersey Sound. It's the music of Liverpool. Most of us call it English R&B. You'll get an earful of it if you show up at the Jac."

"Do you want me to show up, Gin?" I asked in a small voice.

"I could care less, Yank."

"Why must you always be so hardboiled?"

I decided not to express my hurt feelings as we entered a pub where the smoke, smell of beer, and the sounds of friendly chatter acted as a sort of salve on my sulking.

"What's your pleasure?" I asked as soon as I was seated.

"A small Hodgson." said Gin.

"A small bitter for the lady and a pint of Guinness for me," I said to the bartender.

"This is so fab that the paper is noticing the lads from Liverpool. It's high time, isn't it now? This poor city has been on the brink since the Empire crumbled after the 14-18 war. It's nice to have some positive news for a change."

"We call it World War One."

"Leave it to you Yanks to change the bloody name of a war."

The bartender, who was serving our drinks, said lustily to some nearby drinkers, "Hear that now lads, the guv here is into Scouse Swing."

"Is this Scouse Swing the same thing as the Mersey Sound?" I asked, already knowing the answer.

"Some call it the Mersey Beat," put in another man.

"Yeah, I'm interested in the Mersey Beat."

"Talk to me or you'll have an entire pub full of new drinking companions," whined Gin, turning me around in the stool so I faced her. The expression on her face was the softest I had ever seen on it. Her face was remarkably pretty and gentle."

"I'm only exchanging in a little small talk, Gin."

"Keep your words inward Al, luv. Come back here another time to talk with them. It's me what needs your small talk, not them."

"Okay, my dear," I said grandly.

"When you act the proper gent I rather fancy you myself," she cooed. Then in a flash the softness gave away to hardness as she added, "but I won't stand to be treated like a Rutty Judy, if you catch my meaning."

"I have no idea what a 'Rutty Judy' is."

"Aye, aye, mate. I'll wise you up, seeing how you're just of the boat. Judy is usually a right pretty and proper name when you use it correctly. But around here they use it to mean a slut and I'm not that at all. And a 'Rutty Judy' is a bird what belongs to a street gang. Some of them are mean bitches…and they're violent as well."

"You're not a 'Rutty Judy', its' plain to see."

"And a Judy will do things with any feller who'll have 'em."

"No, I don't think you're a 'Rutty Judy'," I agreed for a second time, my face turning red.

"What's the deep blush for, mate?" she demanded to know.

"You're a nice girl, Gin?"

"Am I, now?"

"I like you."

"Do you like me because you think I'm like one of those easy American birds? Well, I'm not. Let's make that clear from the start, what? I have a mind of me own, you know."

"Don't jump down my throat."

"And don't get the notion you can come sniffing around me whenever you get a gut filled with stout. I'd slam the door in your face or sic the dogs on ye."

"Put a lid on that blab," I said shortly as I waved over the bartender. "Another one for me, but you'll have to ask Joan of Arc whether she wants another one before she embarks on another crusade, for she'll spear me if I ask her even the simplest thing."

The bartender, taken back some, looked surprised before managing a smile and asking Ginny her pleasure. It was suddenly very quiet and still inside of the pub, I guess we were the main attraction.

"Ach now, sweetie pie, don't carry on so," she pleaded with a whisper.

"You started it," I whined back.

"No need for a public scene and all," she growled into my ear, "the people in Liverpool are keen nosey Parkers."

"I hear you," I growled back. Feeling lousy, I frowned deeply into my pint. I was aware that I had overreacted.

"Don't be such a baby, Al."

"We can kiss and make up," I sheepishly suggested.

"Right then," she agreed, offering me her lips.

The kiss was short and pleasant. Our pub room audience turned away back to their own drinks and problems. I wanted to say more, but I knew a person like Gin needed to control the show at their own pace. I was also afraid to lose her smile.

"Good," I said.

"Please say more than that, luv."

"Can I say I like drinking beer with you and kissing your lips? I don't expect any more than that which you want to give."

"Ah, Al, you're not just an artist, you're a bullshit artist as well."

"But what I just said is the truth," I insisted.

"Right you are, dear."

"Will you go to the Jac with me to see the Beatles?"

"Sorry, luv, but Gerry Marsden has already asked me."

"I see."

"I'm off before I'm tempted to slap your sulking face," she laughed, skipping out the door before I could stop her.

"Another pint," I ordered.

"Another pint you'll get, sir!"

With a fresh draft set in front of me, I quickly wormed my way into a nearby conversation and soon I had a roomful of drinking mates. As the pints went down I began to play the role of the man of the world.

"Time, please, gentlemen!" yelled the bartender.

"In America they yell, 'Motel Time.'"

"Motel Time, is it?" asked an old gaffer.

"It means 'finish your beer and take your girlfriend to the nearest motel'," I explained to the delight of the other drinkers. However, I didn't receive any invitations home for more beer, so I stumbled back to my digs, alone.

The next day Mrs. Lampkins was slightly miffed at me for my late night entry. She had told me more than once she frowned upon men who drank at pubs with free loaders. I suspected most of her disapproval didn't arise over liquor, but rather that she resented the way I stumbled by her bedroom door without knocking. Maybe she thought I was better drunk than absent, while I took the opposing viewpoint.

I regretted her coldness because since coming to England my hangovers somehow intensified my sex drive. I don't have any explanation.

Mrs. Lampkins was making all sorts of racket as she went about her morning household chores, broadly hinting that I should get out from underfoot and allow her a chance to tidy up my apartment. I retreated to my bedroom and dug into my suitcase, finally locating my long neglected Kodak camera that had sunk to the bottom.

"Mrs. L, I'm off to take some photographs of Liverpool," I cheerfully said as I made for the door.

"Don't hang back on my account Dr. Moran. I'm quite sure I shall be happy and busy all day and all night...and I'll stay that way for some time to come."

First, I took in the Walker Art Gallery, a building that had been made a gift to the city of Liverpool by one Sir Andrew Barclay Walker, the Lord Mayor of the city in 1873. My headache put me in a mood to reject painting, so I made my way to the Merseyside Maritime Museum, which I enjoy much more. I imagined that some of my Irish forbearers had sailed from Ireland to Liverpool to work on the docks before sailing off to a better life in America.

As the day waned I drifted down to the Albert Docks just in time to board the ferry boat heading to Birkenhead. The ferry boat floated easily across the Mersey River to the other side. The ferry boat was almost empty save for a few people off to work on the other side and a teenage boy lugging along a bicycle.

I walked to the top of the vessel and took photographs of the Custom House on the Liverpool side. I then shot several pictures of the rolling waves and of the approaching shore of Birkenhead.

A young woman was sitting on a bench and I decided to chat her up. A hung-over outsider sometimes has more confidence than a clear-headed homeboy.

"Gray day, huh?"

"Yes, that it is, indeed," she replied in a clip manner, dismissing me with a downward head more interested in her cup of coffee than the likes of me.

I retreated below deck where I remained until the ferry docked. As the other passengers got off, I remained in my seat. What was there to see in Birkenhead, I wondered.

"Not going ashore, sir?" asked one of the boat's crew in a friendly though surprised voice.

"No. I just got on for the ride. I'm just a tourist. I'll be glad to pay extra."

"There's no need to trouble about it sir. Enjoy your stay

here in Liverpool. Beneath it all it's a grand place. Been here all me life, but if they ever stop this old tug's runs I'd probably head for your parish across the ocean. I have a brother in Detroit."

The Liverpudlians are a friendly people.

Later, returning to the Liverpool side, I decided to find the nearest pub and get smashed again. There was no need to keep my head clear if Gin and Mrs. L were both playing hard to get, I said to myself, as I walked up O'Ferrall Street.

I darted into the first pub I chanced upon for a pint and I was greeted by a loud bartender and a bored middle aged couple. The three of them were eyeing a television soap opera. The establishment didn't look like a promising alternative to the Jac Coffee House where Long John and the Silver Beatles would be playing. Even John's insulting personally and Gin's flirting with Marsden had to beat sitting in a dull pub watching an even duller program on the telly.

"Sod it," I grumbled to myself, gulping down my stout, pocking my change and heading out the door without a backwards glance.

It was no use trying to talk myself out of heading in the direction where my heart wanted to go. I entered the Jac to be greeted by the typical English pub smells of beer, smoke, spit and fish n chips. Above the smells rumbled Liverpudlian scouser accents and above this sound rumbled rock n roll music. The din was at first obnoxious, but when my ears tuned in upon the music it was okay. When the song concluded, the audience, mostly made up of college co-eds and classmates, greeted it with loud primal screams. I wasn't sure if it was a scream of pain or rock n roll sexual joy.

I looked up at the small stage to see Lennon with a blue guitar in his hand. On his left George, the gaunt, serious boy and Paul, the dark handsome one. Both were playing guitars. To the far right of John was Stu Sutcliffe, a quiet but immensely talented lad from the Art College. According to Teddy Griffith, this young man had won several art prizes which bespoke of a brilliant future as a painter, that is, if Lennon didn't sidetrack him with the rock n roll fever. Looking up at Stu on stage, the darkness covering half of his face in a moon shadow, it was possible for anybody in the audience to sense the embarrassment that the lad revealed with only part of his face in the light. Even to my untrained eye and ears it was quite clear that the boy could do little more with his bass than strum. I would have placed a wager right then and there that little Stu would rather be painting quietly in his studio than making a fool out of himself pretending to play a musical instrument.

"Get in tune, Stu, lad," Lennon shouted at the poor guy in an audible voice.

Stu visibly flinched.

"Come on over John, I've found a smashing chord to start *Twenty Flight Rock*," Paul, who was giving Stu a peeved glare, shouted to John, who was still busy instructing Stu on how to play his bass. When *Twenty Flight Rock* began it sounded like Stu was playing bass to the previous song.

"Dr. Moran!" called out a female voice.

"Dr. Moran! Over this way, sir!" chimed in a man's voice.

It was Gin and Gerry calling out from a crowded table in the back where they had managed to save me a seat. With a mixture of excitement and regret I took a seat.

"What is your pleasure then, luv?" asked a big blowsy blond whose bouncing breasts looked mighty inviting after a long cold ride across the Mersey.

"Guinness."

"Come again, luv."

"It isn't a boozer here, Dr. Moran," explained Gerry. "We

only serve coffee, tea, orange juice and such."

"They have American coffee here, Dr. Moran," pointed out Gin.

"And what's wrong with good English tea?" the waitress asked with mocked aggressiveness.

"English tea, it is, my dear fine lady," I ordered with a silly grin that I hoped hinted at something more than customer service. Gin's face briefly frowned at my flirting. However, she quickly caught herself and grabbed a hold of Gerry's arm. It was the opening cannon volley of a night of sexual warfare that ultimately saw me blown off the field of combat.

"Ah, Mr. Williams, sir, please!" Gerry suddenly called out to a very short little fellow with a beatnik beard and a carriage that suggested an overabundance of self-importance.

"Aye, mate?" this Mr. Williams spat out in a gruff voice.

"Mr. Williams, I want to prove to you that we're getting a legitimate crowd here instead of the usual rock n dole boys the other places get in the 8 district."

"Glad to hear it, Marsden, lad," beamed Mr. Williams. "Me bloody business could stand an upgrade, as could all the other joints here on Slater, God help us." As he spoke the little man began to stare at me with interest.

"This is Dr. Moran, a lecturer of Art at the college," introduced Gerry.

"I'm Allan Williams, businessman of several tiny local clubs," said Mr. Williams, aggressively shaking my hand. "It's rare indeed to meet an intellectual who fancies R&B on Slater. Usually your crowd hangs about the tonier establishments in Liverpool, listening to jazz."

"Local clubs, is it?" sniffed the waitress, setting down my tea. "Strip joints, he means."

"Hush, fach."

"Tell the professor about your nudie place over on Seel,

the one you operate with that cheesy Lord Woobine," persisted the waitress.

"Yes, I'm really excited by the Merseyside music scene," I cut in to be polite. "It's more exciting than that drab cotton candy junk people like Frankie Avalon, Bobby Rydell and Fabian are cranking out on their records back home."

"Are you a Yank?" shouted Allan. "Are you in the music industry racket by any chance?"

"Music is only my hobby. I'm only an art teacher."

Williams face dropped. "Then you have no pull with any American record labels?"

"Sorry. I'm afraid not."

"Oh well, I'll stand you a cuppa all the same and maybe we'll do business someday, eh Yank?"

"Before you take off Mr. Williams, please give me your opinion as to who has the best band in Liverpool right now," I pestered.

"Rory Storm and the Hurricanes are the best. I have no qualms about saying that, professor. Derry and the Seniors are a close second. After that the local talent falls rather thin."

"Wot about the lads and meself?" Gerry whined playfully.

Allan Williams only snorted a reply.

"What about Long John and the Silver Beatles" I asked, nodding to the boys up on stage drinking coffee, smoking cigarettes and horsing around instead of entertaining the audience.

"A right load of layabouts, they all are in my humble opinion."

"They have some talent, I think."

"Talent in painting the walls of my shit house, they have, that or drawing pints at the nearest boozer. Good lads, yes, who should stick to the chosen professions of their fathers...labor.

Look at 'em up there larking about like a bunch of dole boys. Now I must toddle off sir."

"George will now play some raunchy 5 note blues riffs from Arthur "Guitar Boogie" Smith," Paul breathed into the microphone. "Let's have a nice hand for George Harrison."

"And let's have a nice handout for Lennon and McCartney," Lennon came in with a follow up quip.

The crowd loudly applauded, seemingly to know this "Guitar Boogie" who was probably another talented American Negro I didn't know.

With skill and apparent pain George doggedly made his way through his solo. He's going to be good, I noted to myself, especially if he kept with it which I suspected he would by the bulldog grip he had on the neck of the guitar and the set lock of his jaw.

Ginny began to kiss Gerry all over the face, mouth, neck and hair to my abject anguish. My eyes searched for the buxom waitress. I could tell she was another lost cause when I ordered another cup.

"Look ladies and ladies and lardsies and gentle and mental and metal men, we have a Yank in the audience by the name of Dr. Albert Moran and renamed to my shame Mr. Al Capone from Chicago his home far from Rome. The lads and meself want our favorite Yank to hear our favorite song form Yankeeland. We sing it in his honor. Give us the beat Tommy, son," shouted John.

The drummer, Tommy Moore, forcefully led the group into a spirited version of *Blue Suede shoes*. At that moment I could see that the Beatles, sloppy and unprofessional to a man (except for Tommy Moore, the middle-aged drummer, who was soon to leave the group), could ignite the audience with some unknown electrical spark. Allan Williams, good soul that he might be, had overlooked what was sure to become Liverpool's number one band.

During the group's break John, followed by his troops, came over to the table to greet us.

"Dr. Moran!" called out John, pointing at Ginny, "is the tart doing you wrong?"

"Mind your own business, Lennon," retorted Gin, shaking a 'naughty' finger in reply.

"We won't have you breaking the professor's heart, luv."

"I'm a big boy, Lennon," I mumbled out, embarrassed to have my secret made known to the general public.

"Get her in a punch up and teach her place, mate," suggested John.

"I tried it and lost," I goofed around in return in hopes of smoothing over any rough edges caused by John.

"I fought the Brownie and the Brownie won," sing-songed Lennon.

"Have done with it, Lennon, you swine," snapped Gin, who was getting angry much to John's delight and my chagrin.

"Mr. Williams, Allan, sir," called Paul, whose hollering took away the attention from John's egging on of Gin.

"Eh, lad, wot's all the noise on about then?" snapped Allan, none too keen on the intrusion from this member of a lowly act.

"Meet Dr. Moran, a professor from Chicago, the Windy City, as it is known in the States and the inner blues circles in England because of its great winds," puffed out Paul.

"I've met the gentleman. He's a teacher; he's not a bleeding record man now, is he? Now toddle off before ye cheese me off, son."

"He speaks German," added Gin, finally unwinding herself from Gerry. I couldn't remember having told her that, although it was true.

"Wot's that, then?" asked Allan, turning his head towards

me with a look of renewed interest. "We may still have something here, professor. Speaking the Kraut tongue is an important business commodity in this line."

"He's a right educated man, that Dr. Moran from Chicago. He's famous at the Arty for his unworldly and bookish ways," chirped Paul for no apparent reason.

"And how would you know that son?" John coolly asked. "You were at the Inny the last time I looked."

"I'll be at the Arty soon enough," mumbled Paul, his face turning a shade of red. Many times over the years I have seen how John, with only a few cold and cutting words, could reduce Paul to a mass of inferiority complexes.

"German is part of his vast store of manuscript learning," said John, the words rolling neatly off of his tongue. He had only finished what Paul had started.

"Sudden interest, like, eh, Mr. Williams?" kidded George, grinning.

As Allan went into a tirade about the boys being too nosey, Gerry had the courtesy to explain all the fuss made over my limited ability to speak German.

"You see Mr. Williams here is considering setting up a musical business trip to Hamburg, Germany, where he wants to try his hand at booking club dates for his slate of beat and jive bands back here in the Pool. Outside of a few clubs in Liverpool, one or two national contests, a couple of halls in Scotland and the resort circuit, there's no outlet for us R&B lads. We hope Hamburg will open things up for us."

Gin tugged at my sleeves and whispered in my ear, "Don't have any of it, Al. Williams is a nice enough bloke but he's filling the lads with all sorts of rubbish about how experience in Germany will open doors all over the rest of Europe and maybe even in London. Shut him up, will you."

It struck me as funny that Liverpool bands would have to cross over the English Channel and make it big on the continental side before getting a break in their own land. Although Liverpool is only a few hours' drive from London, it is decidedly the boondocks as far as the Londoners were concerned. The attitude in London was that nobody of any importance came from the North Country save comedians who talked with silly accents and wore funny hats.

"Do German words come easily out of your mouth, Dr. Moran?" asked Mr. Williams.

I made my reply in undoubtedly rotten Germany but it was enough to impress my private audience.

"Book learned?" Allan asked with dark suspicions.

"Some of my German was learned from books," I confessed. "I had two years in high school and three years at the university."

"He has his O levels in the Kraut language, I tell you" John insisted in a holler.

"But can you do it on a practical, real life basis, like," Allan persisted, all ears.

"He means, can you talk it like with real live Germanyland natives, Dr. Moran," deadpanned George.

"Can you order a bleeding lager in German?" tossed in Lennon.

"My grandparents on my mother's side were born over in Augsburg and they always spoke it to one another in the house, so my brothers and I learned how to speak it. Our neighborhood in Ravenswood was predominantly German, so I grew up with it."

"There you have it, Mr. Williams," laughed John.

"I was able to get along with the language when I was stationed over in Stuttgart for two years," I said, trying to sell myself when it didn't even occur to me why I was.

"Stationed?"

"Our Dr. Moran was with the squaddies over in Krautland, a soldier, like, and real fighting man," snapped John. "He was a shorthaired G.I., like Elvis."

"Would you go to Hamburg with me to strike a deal or two?" asked Allan, adding, "Of course, you'd get a percentage if there's a profit."

"I'm a teacher, not a music promoter, Mr. Williams."

"It would do all the lads a great turn and all," said George, gently appealing to my sense of comradeship.

"Fair go, mate," pitched in Paul.

"The man doesn't want to go to bloody Germany, so have off, will you," growled John, going all hard to prove that he didn't give a damn.

"Hamburg is but a short jaunt from here, Dr. Moran," continued Mr. Williams in a relentless fashion.

"Plenty of lovely ladies with nice blond hair and blue eyes like Marilyn Monroe, waiting for you to pull," tempted George.

"And big knockers like Marilyn as well," sneered John.

"Lennon!" protested Gin. "I'm sure Dr. Moran isn't at all interested in that sort of goings on or that kind of girl."

"Are you so certain about that, honey?" launched John. "Well luv, maybe you do at that seeing how you two are such good mates and all."

"Piss off, you rotter!" Gin angrily said, huffing off to the ladies.

During this brief episode Paul grabbed my arm and said earnestly, "Please Dr. Moran, an educated American like you could open doors for all of us working lads here deserving a shot at the big time. If this production works out, as is likely if we play it through, there could be heaps of quids to go around for the lot of us. Big dosh, like. Maybe not 'big' as in 'big' American showbiz style, but big Liverpool style. It could help keep a lot of us British lads off the dole, now wouldn't it then? It surely would help a chap make his car payments and help deal with the council house mortgage. We could also be better able to assist our folks, grandparents, da, so on. Have a good think on it, will you. We shall not forget a mate who came through for us in the pinch. We Beatles are as loyal as can be. Besides, if I earn me one hundred pounds I can retire in style.

"Allan, I'll go to Hamburg with you sometime to do the translating for you, but we'll have to go over a weekend or during a school holiday because I can't do anything that will interfere with my teaching duties."

"Christmastime it is then, right o?"

"Maybe Father Christmas will be good to us Liverpool lads this year," prayed George.

"We've all been 'specially good this year 'cept for Johnny," joked Paul.

"No doubt your bleeding Father Christmas will only wank us off," concluded John but not meanly.

Everybody appeared to be happy and the Beatles went back to their gig with zest. Gin resentfully went back to attacking Gerry. I went to a game of solitaire.

CHAPTER SIX

After that evening at the Jacanda Coffee House, John Lennon began to visit my classes more frequently. Perhaps he attended enough classes to learn a few facts and techniques for his future endeavors as an artist. However, I strongly suspected he attended just enough to keep from flunking out. Failure would mean he'd lose his grant and be forced to earn a living. Although his behavior was never that terrible, it still bordered on the rebellious. The assignments he turned in for grades were usually never much above the mediocre. Overall, he was just doing enough to pass, nothing more.

Later some claimed that Lennon had been a promising artist who was destined to become a great painter or illustrator; this is far from the truth. No way in hell was Lennon a superior artist. Although it is true Lennon never made much of an effort to much more than fall off of the fence into the safe side of passing, it was quite evident to me that his abilities were nominal. For all his nastiness I truly liked the boy. Fair being fair, even at his best John Lennon's artwork always leaned toward the bottom of the class.

One distinctive point about Lennon's work was that he had a slug hammer hard attitude about handicapped people. Piece after piece depicted pathetic cripples of all sorts caught in the most difficult and obscene situations. One could state that his attitudes towards lost souls were a fetish or an obsession. His countless drawings of lame old men, poor souls in wheelchairs and children on crutches were disturbing. His nightmare dwarves and elfish goons, with their deformed hunched backs and twisted faces, stared at one with the intensity of burning cinders. I couldn't relate to his fixations nor could I enjoy them, thus his grades were weak. But I did not want to be the one to cost this appealing enigma of a man to lose his scholarship.

"You're a Greenwich Village intellectual rebel, Dr. Moran, aren't you?" John quipped one day after class.

"I'm from Chicago's Olde Town, not New York's Greenwich Village," I replied.

"So then a real live American beatnik like yourself should have more appreciation of the sublime."

"You need more substance and less sublime," I shot back.

"Maybe I should turn in drawings of naked men with big cocks, like our Ginny Browne."

Gin, who was standing nearby, turned a shade of bright red. She gushed, "I hate you, Lennon. I swear I do."

"Go gentle with us, sweetheart."

Before Lennon could get in another word Ginny turned on her heels and stomped away. She seemed to be forever storming away from Lennon and I.

"Now, Lennon, this is a college, not a pub in the 8 district. You should mind your language better than that," I chided him.

"I've seen enough of that one's work to know she's bloody obsessed. I'm right, I telling you."

"Maybe, John, but it's better to be obsessed with the normal than the abnormal."

"Well said, Dr. Al Freud."

I had to laugh at my own graveness.

"You win John. Even still you must try to get her goat all of the time."

"It bothers you, Al. I mean Gin, serious and all. I see it mate. Don't turn red, son. We're mates, to an extent, right enough. She's a tad daft, but hang on and she'll come around."

"Gerry Marsden is more suitable for her I should think," I said, thinking of the large penis on her picture of the 'Faceless Man' assignment. Immediately I regretted spilling the beans to a student of mine.

"Nah, Geoff Mohammed is the one she's on about these days."

"She moves along very rapidly," I remarked, feeling myself turning red again.

"Well, I'm off to sing at Teddy Griffith's Life Session Class."

"I've heard about this thing but where is it?"

"The Life Session, you mean? It's in Room 71. Please come and have a peek, sir."

About an hour later, I entered Room 71 to have a look. There were about fifteen or sixteen students lounging around, easily sketching one another, chatting and sipping tea. It was casual and relaxed. In the middle of the room Lennon was playing his guitar and singing an American folk song called *Hey Joe*. It could have been a scene lifted directly from an episode of Dobie Gillis one of America's hipper television programs.

Teddy hailed me.

"Al! You're interested in checking out our Life Session characters?"

"What's the big idea, Teddy?"

"The idea is to stay relaxed and to draw natural things. You should take a look at June Furlong's painting of this class; it's gear..er, great, I should say. She's working on a portrait to show off John Lennon. Does the cocky lad justice, she does. You seem to rather like the chap, Tony Curtis hairdo and all, I think, so have a look. Thank goodness he's not wearing a pink shirt or those awful drainie pants."

I crept up behind June as not to disturb her. However she felt my presence and spun around with a degree of annoyance. Flustered, she blurted out, "Oh, then it's you sir."

"Carry on, Miss Furlong, it's looking great," I said, not lying, for her drawing of Lennon was excellent.

"Oh, it isn't so much really," she responded with modesty, but pleased all the same.

Not wanting to interfere with her creative process I moved on. There was a comfortable, homey feeling in that room. It had the dual flavor of being coffee house beatnik and tea time British.

"Have a seat Dr. Moran and have a cuppa," shouted Lennon, who appeared pleased to see me again.

The term ended and the Christmas holidays began. The sot-blackened buildings and terraces of redbrick houses of Liverpool were given a cheerful makeup of Christmas lights and decorations.

My students, passing grades in toll, went back to their family homes to celebrate. I lost sight of Ginny Browne for the time being.

Mrs. Lampkins, my landlady and off-on lover, was busy chasing another lodger, a rather crude and vulgar Australian by the name of Smith who was in Liverpool on some sort of engineering job. Though the Aussie was indifferent Mrs. L. was determined to punish me, so she kept up her efforts, leaving me with ample time to wander the streets around the Albert Docks and downtown Liverpool and to feel my loneliness. The highlight of my week were listening to the Goon Show on the BBC radio and going pub crawling. My pleasures were simple and earthy.

On Christmas Day I plied myself full of Guinness Stout so I could sleep through the day and bypass my attack of homesick blues.

New Year's Eve of 1959 came and went with little fanfare on my part. I was wondering if I should return to the States as soon as my contract expired in order to sort myself out.

It was a snowy evening in early January of 1960 and I was walking down Seel Street. I was at the end of my rope in regards to my loneliness and sexual frustration when I happened to pass by what I took to be a strip joint. I examined the posters of the scantily dressed girls and wondered if the pound note entrance fee was worth it. The sight of female flesh sent a feeling of warmth through me that made me believe that the shilling would be well spent.

The Blue Angel was a dreary, dank club in the cellar of an old warehouse. The place was reasonably well-filled with a mixture of businessmen wearing suits and scruffy old men in long tattered trench coats. It was almost too funny to be true.

Up on the stage a woman was a stripper. She was more than a little bit past her peak performing days and running too fat. She removed her bra to reveal her breasts that were still large and firm. It was the flab around her belly that revealed her age. Nonetheless, her body was good enough to make me ache all over. Smirking to myself I wondered if I should do like the rest of the audience and stick my hand below the table. Two things slammed down my desires: first, I noticed Allan Williams, the little Welsh owner of the Jac, urgently making his way towards me; second, I noticed that to the far right, almost out of view of the main act, four bored young men were picking away at their guitars without the benefits of a drumbeat. The four bored young men were the Beatles! And the sounds the lads were putting forth were truly dreadful. The noise was compounded by the fact that they had no drummer to smooth over the rough edges of their guitar music. The boys' lack of spirit didn't help at all.

My heart sank when it dawned upon me that at any moment Lennon would see me and begin to make jests at my expense. I could hear it now, "Gentlemen of the genital, I'd like to point out with my natural hard on the Yank who's moaning in the last row." I also felt uneasy about running into Allan Williams in a strip joint.

"Good evening, professor."

"Good to see you again, Mr. Williams," I mumbled, my face turning its usual shade of red under such circumstances. I was gratified for the darkness of the club.

"So you finally found me, eh? I've been looking for high and low for you since your school term ended. I had hoped to carry you off to Germany with me as my mouthpiece. Where have you been sir? In hiding or what? Who told you I owned this place?"

"I heard about it in a pub," I lied, happy for an escape.

"We've only just opened up on these premises."

"I guess I just stumbled upon it by chance."

The stripper finished her act and slipped off stage to horny applause.

"But I really never expected for you to come down into this dive. Don't judge me too harshly on this run. Right sad, really. A wanking-off station for the frustrated and the perverted. Ah, never mind all that, then. They're all poor souls who have mothers as well as any chapel goer and there's no denying it."

"We all have to get by somehow, I guess."

"You're a tolerant man, Dr. Moran, as I gather most Yanks are. Oh, by the by, later on I'd like for you to meet Bruno Kochsnider. As you can surmise from the name, he's a Kraut from Krautland. A real Nazi Hun at that. Anyways, in a few days he's coming out here to Liverpool to book bands for his Kaiserkellar Club back in Hamburg. Maybe the goose stepper will show up any time now. Maybe it'll be tonight. Who knows?"

"So you don't have to take me to Germany now?"

"I have already gone and returned," snapped Allan, beginning to fume a bit. "I dragged me arse over there with some tapes to play for Bruno the Kraut and what happens when I turned on me bleeding tape machine? Noise! That's what the tape had on it! Bleeding noises! Gits! Gits making noises like pigs, dogs, horses! You name it, they did it! They did everything but their own music. And here I'm trying to help them get wot's due to 'em."

"It was a waste of your time, Allan?"

"Too bloody right! I fancy Lennon sabotaged the whole thing as a lark. Now look at the great Lennon and his flipping

Beatles! This will learn 'em to look at whom they're mucking about with. Serves 'em right, it does."

"But this is no place for boys their age, Mr. Williams," I protested. "For Pete's sake Paul and George are still in high school."

"Keeps 'em out of the goal, doesn't it?"

"They deserve better than to play in a strip joint."

"Do they, then? Who'd have the lot save me? And this will teach them to know when a joke is being carried too far. I reckon a few gigs here be taming their wild natures a wee bit."

"That or it'll break their spirits."

"Don't be a Father Flannigan about them, sir. Besides, the lads have no drummer and none of the dance halls will have 'em on. They had Tommy Moore, a right good skin beater too, but Lennon drove him off with his slagging."

"I wish I could help them out with the drumming, but the only thing I can play is the radio."

"If you can master the drumbeat in a few weeks I'm certain I could book the lads a week or two on a tour of clubs up in Bonnie Scotland. Pays eighteen pounds, it does. The Jacques are that keen about our beat and jive bands."

"Eighteen pounds a week is pretty good wages for an English working lad."

"Nah, that's eighteen pounds for the whole bloody band," corrected Allan.

I was about to remark on the injustice of the wages when the four Beatles trooped over to the table and took seats. Gone was their usual spirited ways. Oddly enough they were very subdued and appeared to be genuinely pleased to see a friendly face in this crowd of misfits.

"Ah, you have come here to this grotty place to see us working with this lot, have you?" asked Paul, speaking with false cheerfulness to help dispel the gloom of the gathering.

"You're lucky to be working, so shurrup," hissed Allan.

"We need a bloody drummer, we do," put in George.

"We need another gig away from here," complained Stu against better judgment.

"We need a bloody bass player before we can get another gig!" Lennon ate up Stu. George and Paul glared at Stu, no doubt inwardly relieved that John was attacking him and not them. Poor Stu visibly reconciled from the burning flame of the trio's joint rebuttal.

"Mr. Williams, can't you find us a drummer?" asked George.

"Are drummers so hard to come by in Liverpool as all that?" whined Paul.

"Maybe you chaps better get on your hands and knees and crawl to that Tommy Moore bloke with his nice and new drum kit and beg him to rejoin your rag tag band. After all, not only is his set all new and such, but he can beat out a tune as good as the next drummer in this town," suggested Allan, enjoying the misery of the boys.

"He's also thirty-six years old, the fucker is. That's too fucking old to be in a rock n roll band. Even Dr. Moran here is younger than your blessed Tommy Moore. He can keep his fork lifting job at the bottle works," said John.

"Thirty-six is old for a musician unless you're American, that is Dr. Moran," Paul said sweetly.

"I'm not a musician, but thanks all the same," I answered with a smile. Paul was the biggest suck-up of the lot.

"I wish you would have kept on walking down Seel Street and passed us by," chirped Stu, trying hard to belong to the group by acting like he felt the most miserable. It was foolish for the boy to be wasting his time with the others who were truly rocker.

"You little git, he's here to stare at the big tits and not to listen to you fuck up simple chords," snapped John.

"Well, that's only partially correct John. I don't mind having a look at the girls as well as see you guys and wish you all a 'Merry Christmas'." I said.

"Not much of a way to spend your Christmas holidays what, Al?" John said with some show of sympathy.

Before I could think of another lie to save face Allan came to my rescue by saying, "You're both bloody wrong, the man's after coming here to help me speak to that nasty Nazi about booking the lot of yours dates in Deutchland."

"Allan," the boys chorused in an excited harmony. It was the best sound they had made all night.

"When can we go to Hamburg?" asked George.

"What cheek, eh?" laughed Allan, playing hard to get. "And you not old enough for a work permit George."

"I'll bloody lie to get one," retorted Harrison.

"Allan, you bastard, you mean to let us rot here in your nudie den?" protested Stu.

"Easy, Stu, you'll give the dirty bugger a stiffy if you argue with him. I know his fucking game. Bleeding nudie it is for us until the gift has a change of heart," said John, his voice sad. He took the cigarette out of Stu's mouth and stuck it in his own.

"Maybe I'll do you a favor and get you a blinking booking if you find yourself a blinking drummer," repeated Allan.

"We've looked all over Liverpool for one of them but apparently they aren't making them these days like they used to," countered Paul.

"Break time is over! Let's get those cocks grinding!"

Allan went back to his customers as the Beatles reluctantly shuffled back to their set. Only Lennon lingered behind.

"It were the ladies that bought you in and not us, eh,

right? Own up to it, professor. Only natural, I should think. It can't be easy being a bachelor in this town," Lennon said almost kindly. I didn't know how to respond as I never really trusted John's outward appearances of kindness.

"I got sick of the pubs."

"Did you, then?"

"Ah, piss on you, John. Yes, it was the ladies that beckoned me here. It doesn't demote me down to the level of most of the customers here, does it? Besides, it is good to see you all. But I can't help but think that maybe you and Stu belong back at the Arty where there's some hope of developing a skill to earn a living."

"Don't preach to me, Yank. Besides, it was Stu's pictures that won all the prizes and are hanging at the Walker, not mine."

"Right you are, Tommy, so you keep him here for this life."

"Shurrup, will you? Anyways, Tabby wot's her name is on break now and she has a good soul," said John, nodding towards the big breasted blond over near the bar who was nursing a drink and looking bored. "Really, she's a friendly sort, not like our Ginny the tart. This one will go."

"Lennon!" shouted Allan. "Toddle on up to the stage!"

"She zeroed in on your heart, our Gin did," teased John. "Maybe Tabby will take your mind off of things for a while. She's a bit of a whore but don't mention money. She has her pride that one does. I grant the lass that much. Stockings over whiskey ought to do nicely."

The next dancer made her entrance. She was another big busted blond with an aging body. The Beatles began with another round of blatant noisemaking. Stu and John sounded particularly rotten. Paul was too much of a pro to do his sulking through his sound, so he put forth some effort. And Harrison was using the striptease stint as valuable time to hone his craft. I walked over to Tabby's table.

"May I buy you a drink, Tabby?" I asked.

"Bugger off, mate."

"My friend, John, thought I should buy you a drink. Sorry if I disturbed you."

"Who's this John bloke?"

"Him," I said, pointing out Lennon.

"Oh, that one, is it? And he suggested you buy me a drink, did he? He's a nice lad for all his blab. And smart, I wager. Between you and me, mate, he's a college man. He's a top scholar."

"He does talk too much, that John and I should know, seeing how he's a student of mine at the Arty."

"So are you a teacher of art, lover?"

"I'm a lecturer at the Art College."

"What is a professor doing inside of this kip? Fancy that, now! Isn't that nice? You were mentioning a drink, weren't you, luv? Seeing how you're a man of letters I suppose I can see my way into letting you stand me one. Let's order us both nice drinks and you can keep me company."

After several stiff drinks the beer goggles slipped nicely over my eyes and Tabby began to look like Marilyn Monroe in her prime. I hadn't had any sex in maybe two months, so I was willing to pay any price.

"When do you knock off for the night?" I ventured.

"You're a nosey Parker, aren't ye, guv? What time would you have me knock off?"

"Right now," I dared.

"Cheeky you are, ye saucy boy."

"We can buy some beer and scotch and go over to your place for a few."

"Now that you mention it, professor, I think I am finished

just now and I could use some grub. And I do need my rest as I am a performer and the stage isn't easy on me legs. Perhaps some drinks with a nice bloke will help me relax, like."

"Maybe in the morning we can go into town and do some Christmas shopping. I need some socks and I can treat you to a few pairs of nice nylon stockings."

"You have some nerve Yank, trying to pick me up like I were a common street whore. Who do you think I am anyways?"

"If I thought you were a whore I would have offered money. Seeing how you're a dancer I only assumed you could always use stockings."

I began to be afraid that I had blundered an opportunity but when she took my hand I realized my line had connected.

Tabby and I spent the night together. By noontime the next day we had gone our separate ways. By six o'clock in the evening I was sitting all by myself in a pub and nursing a pint of black n tan.

CHAPTER SEVEN

Only a few days later, with the spring term only a few days off, I chanced upon John Lennon walking down the street in that curious slouch of his.

"Lennon, why aren't you in the South of England on a banker's holiday?" I called out from behind him.

His smile was pleasant but his words were harsh. "Bugger the South of England. It's the dear dreary North for the likes of me. How's 1960 treating you thus far, Dr. Moran?"

"No complaints thus far. Have time for a cuppa?"

"That's a spot of tea in Woolton, mate," hooted John. "I'll turn you into a proper bloody Englishman yet, Al."

"Then we'll have a spot of tea, my good chap. It's on the Arty."

"On the Arty, is it? Well, since we all know your salary makes you a rich man I'll take you up on the cuppa."

The tea and sandwiches went down very well and Lennon appeared to be in a mellow, happy mood. There was nobody around he had to impress with his wit or to torment. He appeared to enjoy my companionship.

"Let's say we catch the 71 and ride over to me Aunt Mimi's place in Woolton? She'd be out now and we could have a private."

"I was on my way to my office."

"It can wait until tomorrow, Al," he almost whined. "Besides, this is business because I want you to take a look at my drawings."

"Are these the ones you turned in for grades?" I asked slowly, for I had no desire to look at them again. Lennon's drawings always depressed me.

"Nah, mate, these are new. It's from me private stock," he

said, adding, "And I have some poems as well."

"So you're a poet as well as a singer and artist?"

"And, too, there are some lyrics I have written."

"What is this about lyrics?"

"Wot is this then? Repeat after John time or what?"

"I can see you being a rocker but I can't imagine you writing poetry."

"And you don't look like the sort of bloke who would teach at an art college. You look more like a bleeding accountant. You could even pass as an advert salesman."

"No offense meant, John. It's just that by appearance you're more of a writer of a rock n roll song than of poetry."

"Writing a poem is like writing a song."

"Where's your aunt's place again?"

"It is over Woolton's way."

"I thought you lived around Gambier Terrace with Peter."

"Sometimes I nod around Gambier for a night or two. All the Arties live there once in their life. But I keep my suitcases and such at me Auntie's house for safe keeping. Woolton is dreadfully proper, but it's quiet. Really, it's all only a short jaunt from here. Come on then, let's have a go at it."

On the bus trip, we passed we passed a rather medieval-looking building which was trying to masquerade as a school.

"I misspent some years in that tomb."

"Looks like a reform school for the hard cases."

"Ho, ho, ho that. Good one, that. No, not quite mate. More like a retarded hospital for the nut cases. I know what I want to do with me life and none of me ideas came from the teachers there. It's in here," he said, tapping his head with this forefinger. He stared at the building until it passed from sight."

"What's the place called?"

"Its' called Quarry Bank High School."

"Didn't McCartney tell me that you guys had a group called the 'Quarry Bank Boys', or something on that order?"

"Funny one, that. Nah Al, your memory is f...ed up. We were the Quarrymen, plain and simple. It was during the short lived skiffle craze."

"Skiffle craze?"

"Is this more 'repeating after John', Al?"

"Hell, I've only been in Liverpool for a couple of months so my knowledge of the local history is hazy at best. So tell me about this skiffle craze. I'm all ears."

"Skiffle was big a few years back, but it's gone with the dinosaurs now. It consisted of band members playing folk guitar, tea chest, broomstick strings and washboards. The lads used instruments of Karl Marx's bloody working class! We used things we could pinch from our Mums' closet. Lonnie Donegan got it all started in maybe, let's see, 1957 but the style didn't last long, perhaps two years at the most. It was great laughs while it lasted, but the sound was dodgy."

"You English sure love your music."

"It's the Irish and Welsh in our blood that makes us Liverpudlians the singingest folks in England. In a few years the West Indians will have their music absorbed into our style so our style will become more black and bluesy."

"John, I think you may be wrong on that point. The genuine blues sound comes from America. It's our homegrown art form, just like jazz."

"Wot's that then?" John asked hotly, angered that I would dare confront him on anything.

Lennon sulked in silence.

We got off the bus and began to walk down Menlove

Avenue. I was taken back at how successful and well-groomed the neighborhood looked, what with its large two-story houses and well-cared for gardens and lawns. This wasn't the dreary rows of council houses one found in working class Liverpool. There were no signs of poverty in Woolton.

"Woolton has a pretty face, doesn't it?" asked John, as if reading my thoughts.

"It's a far cry from the Dingle," I remarked, recalling the name of Liverpool's worse slum.

"I was born in the Dingle," John said softly. "This place in Woolton is me Auntie's and it's not my true habitat."

"I see."

"Me da was a sea chap who had no business in Woolton. He married me mum during the big war. That's when I entered the bloody world by the way of the Dingle. Me Da jumped ship somewhere, maybe in Australia or Chicago, and we haven't heard from the swine since. Alf or Freddie were his name."

"That's tough luck."

"Piss on him, the farty git."

"How did your mother get on after he left?"

"She remarried to a Taffy, a Welshman. I was packed off to me Auntie's for safekeeping. Then me Mum died. Hit by a truck down the road a ways. Imagine, she was killed only steps away from me Auntie's doorsteps."

"I'm sorry, John."

Lennon shrugged his shoulders.

John put on the tea kettle and, finishing that, ran upstairs as if to fetch something. I could hear him fumbling through some dresser drawers.

"Where are they off to?" I heard him cry out. "If she's tossed them out I'll toss her out. Ah, here we go then. Hello. Here are my precious creations. Well that's some of them but where the rest get off to. Ah, hello there me pretties Come to poppa. They're all mine, I tell you."

"I'll pour the tea," I called up to him.

"Righto," called down John.

I was filling the cups when the back door opened and in walked a tall, thin lady wearing a long overcoat and a white hat perched on top of her head. She has startled to find a complete stranger helping himself to tea inside of her kitchen. Her expression made me realize she thought I was a burglar on my tea break.

"Hello, miss," I bumbled along for an explanation as a somewhat phony smile began to cross my face. "I'm a friend of John's, that's Mr. John Lennon who lives here."

"Don't you think I know that John Lennon lives here?" the woman literally barked at me. "After all, isn't the boy my own nephew?"

"Ah, yes, he told me he stayed with his aunt."

"And my nephew won't be staying here much longer if he doesn't get busy and improve his marks at the art college."

"I'm sure his marks will improve if he applies himself."

"If they toss him out of the art college because of his poor efforts I'll teach him what for by tossing him out of here."

"I'm sure that won't happen."

"And why do you know so much about my John?"

However, before I could come up with a response the aunt cut me off with, "I should think you're rater too old to be a friend of my John. You're an American, I take it. And why are you so certain he won't be thrown out of school?"

"I know he won't be thrown out of school this term because his grades were good enough to pass my two classes," I said cheerfully, desperately trying to get on the woman's good side, although her abrasiveness wasn't much to my liking. She struck me as the type of person who would snap off a person's head no matter what that person said or did. It was easy to see the source of John's rebellion.

"Aunt Mimi, is that you just now, then?" Lennon called down in a nasty tone of voice.

"There's no need to shout in this house!" she shouted back.

"Sorry, luv," John said falsely.

"Please be so good as to come down here this instant and tell me who this strange man is and why he's drinking my tea."

"I'm Dr. Moran," I said rather stiffly, weary of the woman's rude bluntness.

I would have said more but John cut me off by yelling, "Be nice to Dr. Moran, Auntie. He's me prof from the Arty and he's a ripping good prof I should think."

"You're a professor, are you?" demanded Mrs. Smith, a small degree of respect entering her voice. Over time she had learned to become suspicious of John's choice of companion.

"Yes, miss."

"And you're larking about with the likes of him? What on Earth for?"

"He wanted to show me some of his works."

"Works! Bah! Trash, if you ask me…Dr. Moran."

Lennon huffed into the kitchen and angrily snatched his cup of tea off of the table while he fixed his aunt with a fierce glare. Aunt Mimi, standing her ground, returned the hardness. Apparently the two were immersed in some long running battle of wills. From my viewpoint it looked like a standstill.

"Thank you for serving up tea for me, Dr. Moran," John said sweetly as he shot an annoyed look at his aunt.

"Well," the aunt said simply.

"Well, indeed," intoned John. "I thought you were off for the day so I invited me teacher over for tea. No harm in that, is there? He's been kind to me and has bought me lunch on one or two occasions."

Mrs. Smith frowned at me, barking, "Don't be feeding this boy. I give him plenty to eat but he spends it in the pubs with his no account friends."

"They're me mates, if you please," snapped back John. "And they're me rock n roll band as well, now aren't they then?"

"Rock n roll, rock n roll that's all we have here at Mendips is rock n roll."

"Did Elvis have to put up with such torment?" John addressed me for his aunt's benefit.

"Don't start on Elvis again," pleaded Mrs. Smith.

"Elvis is a great man!" exclaimed John. "Isn't that so, Al?"

"He seems to be a very nice guy too, from what I have read about him in the papers," I pitched in. Truth to tell, I didn't know whether Elvis was a nice guy or not.

"See, I told you so, Auntie, luv," John declared with an air of victory. He enjoyed having his aunt at a disadvantage.

"Elvis Presley may be a nice man, but I don't want him for breakfast, dinner and supper."

"You'll whistle a different tune when the Beatles become as big as Elvis. I'm getting right good on guitar, if I do say so myself."

"The guitar is alright as a hobby, John, but you'll never make a living from it."

"We'll see about that," John grumbled darkly, slapping a stack of drawings into my hands. "Ignore her and have a look see over me bloody art, Al."

Sidestepping John's hostility, Mrs. Smith crept up behind

me to have a peek over my shoulder at John's collected works.

"Let's hope there's steady salary somewhere in all this scribbling just in case the guitar business doesn't come through, Dr. Moran," she said firmly, attentively scanning at the pictures as I thumbed through them. I could sense that she was examining my face for my reactions towards the various pieces. The longer she stared at John's works the more doubtful her own face looked. For all her harshness, the woman was greatly concerned about her nephew's future. I felt sorry for the old aunt because I knew John had not been an easy cross for her to bear.

"I can always be an illustrator if the music doesn't pan out," John said slowly, his eyes also glued to my face.

The drawings didn't do a thing for me, I'm afraid to report. The pieces were essentially of the same temperament of things he had turned in for grades at school. The same themes he had used for his homework assignments were all there again: handicap people with deformed legs and using crutches. One notably sickening picture was of a one-legged striptease dancer with armless men applauding with their stumps in the audience. The tea inside of my stomach began to make me feel queasy.

"Maybe its art, but I don't see it for that," Mrs. Smith announced firmly with what I took to be sound judgment. At least she hadn't allowed her love for him to overcome her common sense. I respected the woman's realism.

"But what do you think, Al?" pestered John.

"You have a great deal of talent, John, but I guess these etchings don't shed any light on it," I said, trying to soften my criticism. It was how I felt and the aunt was wise enough to see through any lying on my part.

"Don't turn on me too, Al," John said shortly, his face going red before it went stern.

"Your motifs just don't suit my taste."

"Or any other decent person's," tossed in the aunt.

"So you're saying things like this wouldn't sell to the bloody middle-classers like yourself?" challenged John.

"You said it, not me."

At my last remark both the aunt and nephew's faces fell flat. For all their quarrelling and conflict the two of them were counting on John's certificate from the Art College to provide for them in the future. The two loved one another in a fierce fashion and come what may they had thrown in their lot together. The two would be bickering back and forth until one of them died.

"I knew it!" snapped Mrs. Smith, charging back out of the setback. "I wasted my hard-earned money to put you through three years of the Art College and you didn't even learn how to draw a decent normal human being. Illustrator, my foot. Not a soul in Woolton would pay one farthing for this rubbish."

"I'm right sick of you running me down, Aunt Mimi," Lennon shot back. "You've not supported me once in my ambition to be an artist or a musician."

"Not supported, is it?" retorted Aunt Mimi. "Who was it who spent seventeen pounds to buy your first guitar from the Hersey's Store? Who was it lad? I'd like you to tell your Dr. Moran the answer to that simple question. It was me Dr. Moran, that's who."

As the two pounded away at one another I continued to wade my way through Lennon's gallery of handicapped studies until I came across several short poems stuck in between the drawings. Like his visual arts John's poetry was given over to images of the absurd and the silly. I must admit the guy did have an inventive way with word rhyme and play that vaguely reminded me of Lewis Carroll, author of *Alice in Wonderland*, another Brit with a knack for the outrageous. However, a few poems later and I came to the conclusion that John's literary output was rather a lame Beatnik put-on of the likes being written by college students throughout the world. I'm afraid it was too tepid and too trivial to be important...or purchased. By 1960, Allen Ginsberg, Jack Kerouac and Gregory Corso had cornered the market on works about dirty coffee cups and abandoned alleys at dawn. There was nothing new Lennon could add to the genre. But then I came across the third aspect of Lennon's artistic output. It was a tea-stained sheet of notebook paper containing what I took to be the lyrics of a song. The song was simply worded but it had a pleasant, resounding ring to it. I looked at the title of this ditty. It was *Please, Please Me.*

"I must admit, Mrs. Smith," I began, splicing into the heated nastiness of the relatives, "that your nephew does show uniqueness in his poetry."

"Poetry, you say?" asked Mrs. Smith with surprise, cocking her head to read the words off of the paper I was clutching. John beat her to the punch, snatching the sheet out of my hands.

"That's not a bloody poem, man. It's a song, a Beatles' song," John literally howled into my ears.

"Where's your manners?" scolded Mimi, adding, "And what's with all of this Scouse accent about, John? You weren't brought up a little Scouser. You know how to speak properly."

"To be a rocker you have to be black or a working class lad, so you can see my choices are limited."

"Rocker, mocker! If you think you're going to make your fortune with that you've got another thing coming."

John was about to fire back a response when the doorbell rang. "That'd be Cynthia," John declared, abruptly leaving the kitchen.

I felt uneasy being left alone with the angry aunt. I have always truly hated family feuding, especially when it isn't even my own. And the sound of screaming fuzzy English accents had given me an intense headache.

"You'd think that the trip from Holyroke would discourage her, but not that one," Mrs. Smith said hotly.

"Would this be Cynthia Powell?"

"She's the one and the same. Do you know the girl? Ah, yes, you're a lecturer at the Art College, so you've no doubt seen her chasing after my John. Hopefully she's a better student than my troublesome lad, for if they ever get married she'll have to be the breadwinner. He's after following in the footsteps of that Freddie Lennon, his beachcombing father."

"Miss Powell is an excellent student and she has a fine career ahead of her in the magazine art world if she so desires."

"I'm glad to hear that, at least," said Mrs. Smith, her tone becoming milder. "I'm afraid she'll have to earn the bread and butter for the two of them. The way that girl chases after my John I'm sure she'll be in trouble before long. You've no idea how girls these days can't leave off chasing after the boys and some like him not yet a man and out of school who can earn himself a decent living. I'm afraid he's a Lennon and not a Stanley man. We were always afraid he'd turn out like Freddie instead of like our family. Oh Freddie wasn't a bad man, but he couldn't keep his nose clean to save his life."

As though she wasn't given to sharing many confidences with outsiders Mrs. Smith suddenly clapped her mouth shut and barely spoke to me the remainder of my visit.

"Guess who's paying me a visit?" I could hear John's voice approaching the kitchen.

"I have no idea, I'm sure, John. Give us a hint, will you?" returned Cynthia's girlish voice. Her voice was adoring and sweet, like a young woman in love for the first time.

"See here! It's Dr. Moran from the Arty!" exclaimed John triumphantly pointing at me like I was some sort of a celebrity.

Cynthia was taken back, her mouth dropping. Apparently it was uncommon for instructors to be seen inside of the home of their students.

Miss Powell and I exchanged greetings.

"We're regular mates, eh, Dr. Moran?" laughed John, showed off again.

"Cheeky," I laughed in turn.

"I hope I passed all of my subjects," she said demurely. She was a very beautiful, if shy woman. Thinking about Gin, I envied John. What I wouldn't give if Gin would worship me the way Cynthia obviously worshipped John. I wondered how she was spending her holidays.

I absentmindedly said, "You passed of course, and with flying colors."

"More than probably can be said for our John," Mrs. Smith chirped in with a scalding voice.

"Well, John passed both of my classes."

"So there you have it," concluded John.

It was about time to leave. The pubs were opening and I had had my fill of English tea and English family conflict.

CHAPTER EIGHT

It was a slippery night in early March and I was taking still another of my many aimless walks. I made my way down Bold Street and crossed over to Slater Street. I suddenly recognized the entrance of the Jacanda Coffee House. It was a Saturday so I had plenty of time. I decided to drop in for a cuppa and to see how Allan Williams was faring in the music enterprise business.

Allan, who was standing behind the cash register and giving instructions to a young college-aged girl on how to operate the machine, looked up and greeted me with, "Good to see you, Professor Moran. Please come in and have a cuppa."

"I could sure use one on a cold night like this."

"And, hey, those dole boys, the Beatles, are here today taking up valuable space. They wouldn't toddle off to save their lives. Can't you find them jobs on a borstall farm or something?" laughed Allan.

It was true enough; for the four Beatles were taking up needed chairs at a table in the corner. There was one lone cup of tea, now almost empty, sitting in the center of the table, giving the impression that it had been purchased by the combine pences of the foursome and shared in a likewise group fashion.

"What can my girl get you, professor?"

"I want to put in an order in for a coffee and a couple of bacon sandwiches?"

"Your order will be coming right up, sir. Please take a seat."

"Allan?" I called back over my shoulder. "I want to put in an order in for the Beatles."

"If you'd like, sir, but I wouldn't encourage the loafers."

"They'll buy me plenty of bacon butties and coffees in the

future when they wrestle the number one spot from Elvis."

"Don't hold your breath mate," advised Allan.

The Beatles, their ears prickling up at the mention of free food, let out a collective cheer.

"Dr. Moran, you're a lifesaver," yelled John, spotting me first, "and a big peppermint lifesaver at that."

"Tis grand to see you, professor," Paul gushed.

"And we honestly will buy you plenty of bacon butties when we cut our mark," George said in all earnest, taking my off-the-cuff remark seriously.

"Smooth things over with your Aunt Mimi, John?" I asked, starting off on the wrong foot, for his face tensed up. I made matters worse by throwing in, "And I haven't seen much of you at the Arty this term."

John was apparently thinking over what was more important the sandwich or coming up with a nasty response to a stupid question. It took him a full minute before he was able to say through clenched teeth, "I wouldn't know that, now would I, seeing how I haven't seen her in over two months."

"She gave him the heave-ho, like," Paul informed me with a wink.

"Gis a break," snapped John.

"No shame in being tossed out of the house. We're artists, aren't we? And all the time artists suffer," offered Stu, who was glared down by the others for this efforts. He was truly handsome and saintly in a beatnik way.

"We're having none of that suffering for art crop here, Stu," sneered back Paul.

"You can stay with me if you don't have any digs, John," I said gruffly, adding, "Unless you're a fairy, for I shall not put up with any of that rot in my pad."

"Or up your bacon butties, eh?" got off Lennon.

We all shared a laugh. I think the Beatles were impressed by my offer to John. Once again Lennon had gained some adult status in the eyes of his mates through his association with me. Once again too, I was being Santa Claus and liking it as well. Even Lennon was duly impressed by my offer, his eyes searching mine to see how genuine the offer was. I regretted making an offer like that to a student because I wasn't sure how the school administration would react.

"Thanks, whacker, but I have already taken up digs at a place on Percy Street and Gambier Terrace," said John.

"That's after I threw him and his junk out of me place," said Stu. "I needed the space for me studio, like."

Our coffees and sandwiches arrived and the Beatles wolfed down their food as though they hadn't eaten in days. I wondered how they could all be so ravenous when each of them had families to feed them. Searching my mind for some cheap Freudian insights on their psychological behaviors I surmised that the gulping of their food betrayed a natural desire to swallow life down in large chunks. Ha! I put my freshman psychology behind me as I grabbed another bacon butty before it was nicked by one of the lads. The sandwich was greasy but tasty, with a pungent taste that reminded me of salty Liverpool itself.

"Send over more bacon butties, Allan!" I ordered.

"Did you receive a pay increase from the Arty?" John asked with a kind smirk.

"Getting more money out of that lot isn't too likely, Lennon. But speaking of the Arty…"

"No need that. After this term I'm probably out of the place for good. They'll be glad to see me gone, I reckon."

"And you out without you bleeding certificate," Stu threw in John's face, shaking his head with disgust. It was a rare threat to see Stu bait John. Beatle or not Stu was determined to complete his education. As the only son of a working class Scottish-Liverpudlian couple this Stu Sutcliffe recognized the need to earn a diploma to earn a living even if his hero Lennon didn't. I applauded Stu's belief in education and degree.

"Bugger the certificate," snapped John.

"It's important to get on in the world, isn't it?" Stu said firmly, standing his ground.

"You're sounding so petty bourgeoisie these days, Stu," snorted John, anticipating the others to join in the fray on his side.

"And you have no O levels either, Johnny," teased Paul, backing Stu for a change. "Wot's to be done with you, son?"

"Bugger the O's, Paul."

"I didn't know you're being tossed out of the Arty, John," I butted in.

"Not yet, at any rate. But after the spring term I'll lose me grant because of me lousy performance, grade wise. Teddy Griffith and Arthur Ballard have gone out on the limb for me but it weren't no good, so they'll be serving notice soon enough. Oh well, so it goes."

"I'm sorry, Lennon."

"Don't be sorry about anything, Dr. Moran. I'll come out of it okay if Allan will get the Beatles a huge booking over in Hamburg. There's plenty of large clubs over there, American soldiers, squaddies, don't you see."

"There's big money over there," chirped George.

"We can do it!" Paul said with intensity.

"Too blinking right we can do it!" roared John, acting like a cheerleader to his squad.

"Germany's only the first step chaps!" yelped Stu.

"There you go son," encouraged John.

"Then we're off to the stars!" shouted Stu.

"Where are we going fellas?" shouted John, jumping to

his feet.

"To the top, Johnny, to the top!" clamored the Beatles as they also hopped to their feet.

"And where is the top, fellas?"

"To the toppermost of the poppermost!"

"Hey, we'll have none of that roaring in here!" Allan roared himself, coming over to the table.

"Please, Mr. Williams, get us a gig over in Germany," pleaded Paul.

"Please, please me!" added George and Stu on cue.

Only John refused to beg.

"You didn't much appreciate the last job I found you at the Garston Bath," said Allan, his face breaking into a mischievous smile.

"The blood Baths, you mean," corrected George.

"The bloody Tiger Boys almost castrated us for chatting up their bird," reflected Paul.

"We're lucky we got out of there alive, Allan," said Stu.

"And then there was the big skin who wanted to play drums for us. Jesus, the brute mates would have done us if we hadn't let him play," fretted Paul.

"What about the Blue Angel Club on Seel Street, then?" asked Allan, still enjoying laugh, referring to his strip joint.

"No more strip joints as well," insisted John.

"I can't help you lads if you think you're too bloody good to work the average dates in Liverpool," said Allan self-righteously.

"How's about giving us a chance in Hamburg?" dared John.

"We're ready for the Kraut bastards, eh, fellers," put in Paul.

"Ready, me arse!" hooted Allan. "You haven't even got yourself a proper and steady drummer, not to mention anything about how McCartney and Harrison are still mere scholars and not old enough to rate work permits. George here should be in a church choir instead of a jive band. And bloody Stu, bless your heart, should be back in school making something of yourself. And Lennon…well, there's always the dole."

"Just give us over there and we'll figure the rest out ourselves," slashed John.

The next hour or so was spent in harmonious reveling as we sipped coffee and talked too loudly for the other customers. Even Allan got into the spirit of things by sending over a free round of coffee on the house. However, as the evening progressed and the place began to fill with fresh customers with money, it became apparent that Allan wished for us to 'toddle off', as he called it. I must admit I was reluctant to shove off because I was having a great time. The Beatles made me feel young and hopeful. At this point of the narrative I should mention the jolly sexuality that these four Britons were able to create around them wherever they went. It was hard to define. I can't say it had anything actually to do with sexual preference, but I like being with them.

Nonetheless, it was time to clear the table for another group of people no matter how much the five of us hated to leave. I fancied going to the nearest pub for a piss up, but I didn't have the money to stand rounds for four thirsty and healthy young men. Instead, I asked, "Do you guys want to come over to my place now and listen to my records?"

"Lets," said Paul eagerly, looking at John for approval.

"We shouldn't keep you, Al," said John.

"I have no place special to be."

"Time we were out of here, anyway," noted Paul.

"I'd like to get an earful of Dr. Moran's records," pitched in George in that determined bulldog air of his.

"We can pick up some grub and beer on the way over," I suggested.

The Beatles' faces fell.

"You're talking to four very poor lads, mate," John said gruffly.

"I'll stand you all for it," I said, adding just as gruffly, "When you reach the toppermost you can stand me in return. Besides, your company is worth the price."

"Why put up with our company, mate?" John asked suspiciously. "Don't you pal around with Griffith and Ballard?"

"Oh I like them very much, Lennon," I responded, "but they're married men after all and they have lives of their own. I hate to intrude."

"As we hate intruding on you Al," John said softly.

"Please intrude."

"Come on then, wot do you say, mates?" shouted Paul, impatient with John's hard-to-get behavior.

"We're off!" John shouted in turn.

The Beatles cheered in that football team/street gang harmony of theirs as we marched out the door of the Jac.

A light snow was falling over Liverpool as I walked down the street with the Beatles. What a sight it must have been for any average Liverpudlian to see a middle-aged American carefully carrying a bag filled with bottles of ale and stout that were trying to spill out from the ripped bottom of the bag and being followed by four local teenagers clad in black leather jackets and tight blue jeans, who were also carrying bags of assorted groceries.

I ignored Mrs. Lampkins's eardrums as I charged up the stairway to my flat followed by the eight noisy boots of the Beatles. Once inside of my place the din grew steadily louder as the lads expressed delight at my photographs and knick-knacks from Chicago.

"Hello, wot's this, then?" asked Paul, pointing to a large framed photo of my family that maintained a prominent position on my living room wall.

"It's my family."

"What a largish clan you have there, then, Al," said Paul, trying out the 'Al' for the first time.

"How many, Al?" asked Stu, also trying out my first name.

"Count them, stupid," ordered John.

Paul began counting, "One, two, three, four, five, ah that's you Al, seven eight, hey, hello he looks like you, he does, and so does she, and they all look a bit like you, then, nine and ten. Let's see, ten it is, ha!"

"Didn't know you could count that high, Paul," smarted off George.

"Your father must have really fancied your mother," teased John, seeing how I would react to his off-color humor regarding my parents.

"Irishmen make strong lovers, I guess," I said easily.

"Hey, there's a lot of Irish here in Liverpool, like," put in Paul. "Me Da's part Irish, but me Mum was all."

"We're all Irish or Welsh...or West Indian in Liverpool," observed John.

"Me, I'm a Scot," said Stu proudly, pounding his chest.

"Hey, Jacque, how's about making the beans?" ordered John. "Paul, you can manage the eggs and sausage. George, be a good lad and make the toast and pour the ale. Al, you can help me set the bloody table."

Even in a stranger's house Lennon was dishing out the work. The others obeyed without one single complaint. My tiny apartment room soon had a smoky, homey smell of kitchen cooking to go along with the giddy laughter and excited babbling.

"Don't worry about me cooking, Al," said Paul. "I do cooking at our house for myself and the kid brother Michael every day."

"Good deal," I said, pouring out the Guinness and the Bass.

"I've been doing the cooking since me Mum died a few years ago."

"Don't go on about your mother dying when we're having fun, Paul," grumped John, popping open another beer for himself. He had rapidly downed the first beer I had handed him. I hoped he didn't get drunk.

"Sorry that," mumbled Paul.

"It's a party, isn't it then? For Little Richard's sake let's not talk about the dead."

"Aye, right you are there, Johnny."

"Dr. Moran, do you like much butter on your toast?" asked George, still clinging to my formal title and discharging his obligations in all seriousness. He was the youngest of the lot, and his youthful age always became more obvious whenever I was around the Beatles for long. Even while making toast George was all stolid and grave.

It was a tasty though simple one it was: eggs, sausage, toasted cheese sandwiches smothered in beans, and all of it washed down with cold bottles of Guinness Stout, Bass Ale and Hodgson Bitter. We all ate heartily. Not for the first time that day I noticed how Lennon literally tore his food to shreds before swallowing large mouthfuls of food in a noisy and sloppy fashion. He acted as though he hadn't eaten in a month. Surely these manners weren't the ones he had been taught by prim Aunt Mimi back home in Mendips.

Afterwards Stu was delighted to wash the dishes while George dried. The pair of them looked more like dutiful schoolboys doing the dishes for their school master than like hard-edged rockers. Paul scrubbed down the table and took out the rubbish.

John lamely and half-heartily took a few brushes at the floor with a broom. It was the first time that John, in spite of his cockiness, appeared to me to have exceptionally poor physical coordination. He looked completely inadequate at doing even a simple chore like sweeping.

The work all finished, it was then time for the lads to flop themselves down, pints in hand, to listen to my records.

Pure chaos reign as each boy shouted out requests. The Beatles took turns digging through my collection and making their own selections. Needless to say my classical and jazz records were ignored, as were most of my folk and pop LPs. What was wanted was only rock n roll. My attempts to put on Charlie Parker or Dizzy were met with loud vocal demonstrations.

"We'll have none of that horn-tooting tonight," said John.

"If you want jazz you should go to the Cavern. It's all the lot will have," said Stu.

"I played in the Cavern once with one of me old bands and the squares there would have no part of us," said John.

"Hello there, there's some rockabilly here," said Paul, swooping one up and setting it up on my record player.

The four lads almost swooned when the song began to play, much like the way young people would swoon at their own concerts in the very near future.

"That Carl Perkins is gear on guitar," intoned George.

"Wish you had his strumming fingers, eh, la?" laughed John.

"I have me own fingers to strum with, though, don't I, da," retorted George.

"Play some more Carl Perkins, Dr. Moran," pleaded Stu.

"I prefer Roy Orbison myself," I said.

"One day I'll play with Roy," announced George, ignored by the others except for me.

I rose to the status of sainthood when I revealed my stash of Elvis, Little Richard and Chuck Berry. Truth to tell, many of these singles had only recently been mailed to me from my brothers Pete and Frank back in Chicago. Liverpool had made me a true rock n roll fan.

"Do you like Buddy Holly?" asked Paul.

"Did you like Buddy Holly?" corrected John. "He's been dead these past months, hasn't he?"

"Actually Buddy was a favorite of my brother Frank."

"Like, what are the names of your brothers, Dr. Moran?" asked George.

"We have a George, like yourself," I began, "and then there's Frank, Pete and Johnny, like Lennon here. And then there's me of course, Albert."

"That's five, skin," pointed out John.

"Let's see, ah yes, then there's Adam, the oldest."

I put on an album of Buddy Holly singing old southern Sunday meeting hymns and Negro spiritual gospel. The Beatles listened in an awed rapture. I couldn't understand the big deal, for the music didn't hold much for me. It was too alien.

"He's great!" broadcasted Paul, flipping the LP over.

"We want John to wear his glasses whenever we play so we can pay tribute to Buddy, you know what I mean. But our John is having none of it. Isn't that right, Johnny?" teased George.

"Maybe he thinks it hurts his image with the birds," cut in Paul. "You know, glasses not being gear and all."

"But the glasses would help our image," pitched in Stu.

"I hate the glasses. It's a vain part on me, I reckon,"

confessed John.

"At least you'd be able to see all the smashing birds in the audience," reflected Paul seriously.

"But would they want to see me? Now that's the bloody and proper question, isn't it then?"

The Beatles whooped with laughter.

It was almost ten when there was a sharp rap at the door. I knew it would be Mrs. Lampkins before I even opened the door.

"And wot's all this, then, Dr. Moran?" snapped Mrs. Lampkins angrily, her hands clinging her nightgown in a tight grasp. In her frumpy, mode, it would have been embarrassing to me if the Beatles knew that Mrs. Lampkins was a sometime lover of mine.

"Hello, there, Mrs. L," I said dumbly.

"Don't hello there Mrs. L me, Dr. Moran! Do you have any notion what time it is?"

"Well..."

"Ask her what's she's going to do about it, mate," called over John.

"Me Mum will put you up if she tosses you out of here, Dr. Moran," joked George, not helping me one bit.

"Have done with it lads, this being serious and all," said Paul gravely. He was the most mature of the group.

Of course Paul was right and the joking died away completely when the Beatles realized that their bantering was gaining me absolutely no points with my ticked off landlady.

"The noise coming from here sounds more like the local pub at closing them than a respectable boarding house."

"I didn't realize we had gotten so out of hand."

"And wot's this, now?" she asked, glaring at the black

leather jacketed Beatles. "Are you after taking up with Teddy Boys, are yer Dr. Moran?"

"Actually they're students of mine from the Art College," I only partially lied, seeing how John and Stu were students at least.

"Too young for that, I dare say. They're too scruffy by half. There are art students, my foot. What is the college coming to?"

"Madam, my name is Stuart Sutcliffe and if you care to visit the Walker Art Gallery you will see my prize-winning picture there," said Stu proudly.

"And many of his pictures are hanging in the front hallway of the school these past months," said John.

"Mr. Sutcliffe here is the college's most promising artist," I said truthfully.

"You don't say," said Mrs. Lampkins, impressed.

"He'll be Liverpool's Rembrandt before too long," said John, for the first time praising Stu in my presence. It was a nice change of pace.

"We were just on our way out, luv," said George with an endearing smile.

"Sorry if we troubled you, Auntie," teased John, pinching Mrs. Lampkins gently on the cheek.

"Go on with the lot of you," giggled Mrs. Lampkins, who rather enjoyed being touched by a handsome young man. In spite of herself I think Mrs. Lampkins found herself taking a shine to the Beatles. The Beatles trooped by here, one by one, each shaking the old girl's hand.

"See you, la," Lennon called out to me over his shoulder.

"Well, I guess your lads are okay. Just a bit too much good cheer. We meant no harm done."

"There you go Auntie," chuckled John. "Gis us a kiss,

then."

"And us!" chorused the others.

Paul, who was charmingly drunk, clapped his arms around my neck and said, "Good one, eh? Teddy Boys, is it? Only yesterday Jim Mac, that's me Da, said to me, 'Bloody hell, you will not have your trousers as tight as his', 'his' meaning our Johnny's trousers. The gaffer went on to say, 'They're Teddy Boy trousers and not only will you not wear them in this house, you won't wear them, full stop. It's a bad thing.' And I asked him 'Why are drainies and winkle pinchers such bad things?'"

As the door closed George called back, "If you fancy having tea with the Gaffer and me Mum this coming sound, gis a call. We're in the book. We live in the council house at 25 Upton Green, Speke."

CHAPTER NINE

I never took George Harrison up on his offer to have tea with his parents, but I have since heard that his parents were nice, sweet people. I regret not having visited them at their home in Speke. If you read any books about the Beatles you'll probably be able to see that George, of all the Beatles, came from the most 'normal' family. I believe this is why George was easily the most stolid and solid of the lot.

For the time being my connection with the Beatles was to break off, as it would through the years that they threaded their way towards the toppermost of the poppermost, to be the picked up later on.

The only Beatles I saw anything of after the impromptu Christmas bash were Stu and John; and I saw rather more of Stu than John who had taken to all together avoiding school except to visit friends or pick up Cynthia Powell.

"It's definite," Stu informed me one early spring morning. "Our John is to be sent down at term's end."

"He'll have to get a job now, and I rather doubt if anybody will want him for his skills in lettering and illustration," I responded sagely, disappointed that Lennon couldn't compromise enough to stay in school and earn his degree so he could qualify for some sort of job using art.

"No worry that; for we're off to Germany soon."

"So Allan finally landed those gigs in Germany, I see. How soon are you off?"

"Maybe some time in April," answered Stu. "No later than June, according to that German friend of Mr. Williams. You know, soon the Arty may be emptied of all its rock n rollers, for blokes like Johnny, Gerry Marsden and myself will be putting our studies behind us to pursue our careers. You'll have to move to Hamburg to earn your keep as a teacher, Dr. Moran."

"Tell the lads I wish them all well," I said, not telling Stu that he was making a mistake trying to follow in John's footsteps. I knew Lennon had enough money to take care of himself, but I also realized Stu's sole ability was art.

"Thanks, sir. Aye, the lads all hope you will visit us over there. In fact, we are counting on it. Maybe you can visit Hamburg over the next bank holiday. John said for me to tell you and to add 'pretty please' on his part."

As 1960 saw the Beatles venture abroad to make their collective effort, the year also saw me making my own ventures. Besides trying to become a better teacher and continuing my pursuit of Ginny Browne, I began dating a proper Englishwoman from London. My new lover was a kindly but rather chilly fashion designer, who was in Liverpool on a special assignment for a large local department store. We drank gallons of tea, took in the theater, went for long country drives towards Manchester, and occasionally dined at the Adelphi Hotel and danced at the Washington Hotel on Lime Street.

Springtime rain gave away to summer's warmth.

The school term ended and my proper Englishwoman and I took a one month visit to Sweden, Norway and Denmark. She had been commissioned to do some freelance work in a chain of Scandinavian stores. I went along to keep her company and to keep a notebook of my impressions of the northern countries for a possible book in the future. Unfortunately, whereas my friend's purse was rewarded by the venture, my pen produced no traveling masterpiece to rival that of Thackeray or Stevenson. The trip only served to break the bank for me. Later, I imagined my companion had henpecked me out of writing anything creative. Perhaps I was wrong but I had come to the conclusion that the proper Englishwoman from London wasn't the proper travelling mate for me. By August I was back in Liverpool drinking pints, while she had moved over to Birmingham and was taking up with a dentist by the name of Mason.

The autumn semester of 1960 was only a few days off and running when I decided to take the Beatles up on their offer of meeting them in Germany. Nothing much was happening for me around Liverpool and my long-planned for vacation to Scotland wasn't scheduled to take place until the Christmas Holidays.

So I packed my bags and headed for the front door, hollering to Mrs. Lampkins, "Keep my digs clean Mrs. L. I'll be back in a few days."

"Mind you keep out of the German rain," shouted back my landlady. "Their rain is much worse than our gentle English rain. It can kill you, it can."

"The rain wouldn't stop me from this banker's holiday."

"Well if you don't mind the rain at least mind you don't pick up anything from any of those Dutch lasses, you naughty boy, you," she giggled, her good nature giving away to sweetness.

In recent weeks Mrs. Lampkins and I had somehow managed to patch up our relationship. However, after a few one-nighters we had both realized that the old passion was gone. Nonetheless, we decided to remain good chums all the same.

I flagged down a taxi and gave instructions for the Lime Street Station, where I was going to begin my journey to Hamburg with a four hour hike on the British Railway to London. For the past few nights I had spent a great deal of time memorizing times and platform numbers, preparing myself for my jaunt to and back.

I was entering the Lime Street Station when a voice called out to me: "Dr. Moran!"

"Miss Browne!"

"You're not leaving us, are you, Al?" pestered Gin, pointing to my bags.

I hadn't communicated much with Gin during the spring

term or over the summer months. I suspected that she had studiously selected her classes in order to avoid me.

"Would you miss me if I left, Miss Browne?"

"Back to being formal, are we, then?" she asked with uplifted eyes. "And yes, I would miss you. Say are you mad at us, luv?"

"It seems you've been avoiding me."

"Gis a break, luv," she teased, quickly adding with a petulant pout, "Do you really like me all that much, my cheeky Yank, or is it all in your mind?"

"I don't know if it's all in my head, but one thing for sure it hurts."

"Foolish man!" she laughed, kissing me full on the lips.

I pulled her close to me. I mashed her warm, full lips and felt her warmth add to the heat of the autumn day.

"You're something else kid," I said, embarrassed because we were putting on a show in the entrance of the station, which was probably the busiest place in the town center.

"Tell us the truth Al. Are you really leaving this place?"

"Maybe," I teased. "It's been a lonely place for me."

"You're very lonely with your dreadful landlady. You're screwing half of the birds in this old port city. I heard you even fancy whores and strippers."

"They were only to take care of a physical need. You're the only woman I have wanted since I reached England. Besides, you were gaa gaa for Gerry Marsden."

We hugged again for no apparent reason.

"Gaa Gaa for Gerry, ho. Sounds like the name of a blinking song, it does. No, Gerry and I are just good mates. Anyway, he's only hot to get on in the rock n roll world with this band The Pacemakers. They're quite good, you know, especially with their own ballads."

"Are they better than the Beatles?"

"Quite," she said, "but don't change the topic to jive, you. Is it too late for you to cancel your return home?"

"For goodness sake, kid! I'm only going to Germany for a long weekend," I said, explaining my route that would take me to Hamburg in the end.

Gin didn't know whether to be relieved, surprised, angry, or all of those feelings mixed together.

She hollered: "You're going to see the lads play?"

Catching me looking at my watch, she offered to treat me to a spot of tea and a sandwich if I had the time. I took her up on the offer and we found a small shop inside of the station. When we received our orders, we talked excitedly, waving about our hands with energy, as we renewed our interest in one another and the Beatles.

"Take me with you, Al," begged Gin, only half in jest.

"I only have but one ticket and I'm too poor to afford one more."

"You are my American roamer."

Maybe later if they make good we can get a group together from the Arty to visit them. We can tell the rector we're taking a field trip to visit the art galleries in Germany."

"Arty farty!" she snapped back. "I don't want to be with those squares any more than I have to. The place has died since John, Stu and Gerry took it on the lam. Besides, I only want to go with you, darling Al, so we can have the Beatles all to ourselves."

"We'll do that someday, I promise." It was another promise I never lived up to.

We sealed the promise with a kiss as the PA announced the platform number and time for the train departing for London.

"Hold on, love," she said, pulling away from me and digging into her purse. In a flash she dug out a battered and stained postcard with pictures of three buxom Teutonic frauleins flashing promising smiles.

The back side of the card read:

9/27/60

GINNY BROWNIE

HAVING A SMASHING TIME IN KRAUTLAND! HAVE A PUNCHUP WITH BLOKES & BLOKESSES AT YE CRACKLE PUB FOR ME. PAUL, GEORGE, STU & PETE SEND THEIR LOVE & PISSES. TELL AL CAPONE OF CHICAGO TO HAVE A LOOK/SEE IN HAMBURG

LONG JOHN SILVER

"Hey, he sends you postcards and me insults," I gripped. "And who's this Pete fella?"

"That would be Pete Best, the Beatles' new drummer," she explained.

"So they finally found a drummer to replace Tommy Moore."

"Pete sat in with them a few times, but he was never available, like, until recently, to be their full time drummer."

"I think I recall him now," I said brightly. "Wasn't he the dark-looking handsome guy with the nice build whose mother owns the Casbah Club?"

"Aye, that's the lad to the bone. But don't say he's good-looking around McCartney, for he's frightfully jealous about his status as the 'cute one' of the group. He fancies himself a real stud, he does. The girls call him the town bull for a laugh. But he's sweet, isn't he?"

A few more words and then it was time to catch my train. And like the many black and white films of the 1940s, I rushed off to jump on the train as my girl waved with her right hand and brushed away a tear with her left.

I felt somewhat forlorn all the way to London. However, my mood began to lighten up on the boat train ride across the channel. And I began to positively sparkle by the time my next train crossed the Netherlands and entered the industrial sprawls of northern Germany. I killed a great deal of time by practicing my high German on the other passengers inside my coach. When my victims wearied of my lousy pronunciation, I passed the minutes by staring out the window and giving myself up to daydreaming.

When I finally reached Hamburg I was still keyed up and feeling full of energy. Thoughts of Gin and the Beatles had fired me up for a month's worth of hot action.

Instinct told me that I would find the cheapest lodgings at a bed and breakfast close to the docks. After paying a few marks for a moldy and damp Deutchland room, I made my way to the closest Guesthouse, the German's version of a pub. In my baby talk English and lousy German I inquired as to the whereabouts of the Kaiserkeller Club.

"Ah, so, sie Reeperboom," replied the bartender, giving me a broad wink. "Und you being a naughty boy das morgen, ja?"

"Nine. Ich bin ein holiday. Looking for friends. Er...minen freudins."

"Freundins Frauleins! I thought so, yes."

Dirty old bugger, I thought, but friendly for all that and his attitude gave me an indication of what I was in for.

I took a short taxi ride to the Kaiserkeller Club but it was still early, not even four PM and the place was almost deserted. Against my better judgment I ordered a great stein of Haufbrau beer instead of coffee. I made my second error when I allowed a small group of tubby workingmen to catch my eye and draw me over to their table.

"Broast tex to your President Kennedy," announced one,

the drunkest of the lot.

"And toast to your wonderful German beer," I countered, not recalling the name of Germany's president.

"Do you like Herr Kennedy?" asked another.

"I don't know anything about him," I answered truthfully, vaguely remembering that JFK was an Irish Catholic like me.

The rounds and toasts began to come and go at a frenzied pace. Before becoming too smashed I thought of the subject of the Beatles' whereabouts.

"Do you know the Beatles?"

"Ja. I know. They're big, ugly insects. Ja. I know. But we have no beetles in Hamburg. Only roaches, ha!"

"The Beatles I'm talking about are a rock n roll band from England."

"Ja. I know. Rock n roll bugs in England but not in Hamburg. Only beer and frauleins here."

"No, I mean the Beatles is the name of a singing band."

"Singing like in a church?"

"Go to Cologne if you want to hear singing in church," threw in another man.

"Big cathedral in Cologne, not here, ja," tossed in still another.

"We don't go to church in Hamburg," shouted the leader." We drink and play, not sing and pray."

"Look, I'm not talking about singing in church!"

"Hans says you must go to Cologne if you want to sing in a church. Here in Hamburg we only pray for a good time, ha."

"No, you got it all wrong, you guys!" I shouted with despair, "My friends the Beatles sing and play rock n roll."

"Das Beatles sing and play rock n roll in der church?"

"No, they play in nightclubs, like this nightclub…maybe."

The men momentarily looked blank until the spokesman of the group slapped his forehead and exclaimed: "Ach de liber, rock n roll! Johnny B. Goode! Elvis!"

"That's the ticket!"

The men nodded their heads, ordered more beer, and started a chorus of some dreadful Tony Bennett song that they mistakenly took to be rock n roll. After the number, and before they could move on to Andy Williams or Perry Como, I once again asked for the whereabouts of my friends. No matter how much I tried, it became apparent that my new drinking mates weren't hip to the local jive scene. Apparently the tub of lard were only aware of the singles on the jukebox.

Fortunately, as the evening approached and my new mates began to stagger off for home, it became quite clear that the place was beginning to fill up with a crowd that was obviously college student dominated.

At that point I was drunk enough to approach a table of male and female college kids, who were sipping mixed drinks and daintily fingering their cigarettes with the bored indifference that they had no doubt copied from their bored American counterparts, the Beats. I imagine these German students were mimicking what they had seen in the movies depicting the 'Lost Generation' of artists, poets and rebels who made up the ranks of the Beatniks. I knew Greenwich Village and Old Town were filled with these copycat intellectuals.

"Do you know the English band the Beatles?"

"What?" one of them managed to ask with an air of boredom. The others stared at me with hallow eyes.

"I said I'm looking for my friends the Beatles," I persisted, coming across like an aggressive American tourist. "They're a jive band from England."

The reaction at the table was negative. One young woman behaved as if I had asked her to sleep with me. Another woman deliberately puffed cigarette smoke in my general direction. The motion of her breath suggested she felt that even her smoke was too good to land on me. The rest of them sullenly stared into their drinks as if seeking an escape route that way. One fellow began to cough in a nasty way, as though he was trying to send me a message to send me on my way. However, drunk as I was on the heavy German beer and still being a friendly frame of mind from the warmth left over from my encounter with the hearty workingmen, I was in the mood to be a pest.

"You don't know the Beatles? Well, you should because they're a smoking beat band from Liverpool! Everybody loves them."

The mention of 'Liverpool' suddenly appeared to catch the attention of one of the people.

"Are you from Livepool, skin?" asked one young man.

"Yeah whacker, I am," I only half lied.

"But your accent is American, is it not?" asked the fellow, his voice filling with disdain.

"I'm from Chicago in America but I currently live in Liverpool where I teach at the Arty, I mean the Art College of Liverpool."

"The Arty!" exclaimed the young man. "We know of it!"

He rattled off something in German to the others who immediately reacted like an electrical charge had just sparkled across the table and into their bodies. The pretty woman who had blown smoke in my face and into her body was now smiling at me.

"Do you know Stu?" the woman asked dreamily. She was now an altogether different person.

"Yeah, I know Stu Sutcliffe. He's a former student of mine. He's a genius, that Stu. Someday he'll be recognized as a great painter. I have seen enough of his paintings to be able to judge his abilities."

The young woman was elated by my words of praise for

Stu.

The young man explained to me, "She's in love with Stu."

"Klaus!" she hollered in a fierce way.

"All the girls love Stu," continued this Klaus, laughing.

"But where is Stu?" I asked. "And where's Lennon and the others? Don't they play in here?"

"No, Yank, this is Bruno Koschinder's top money-making club, so only the top billing groups like Rory Storm and the Hurricanes, Cass and the Casanovas and Derry and the Juniors play here. The lesser known bands like the Beatles and Gerry and the Pacemakers play over at the Indra Club."

"You make it all sound so dreadful, Kraus," complained Stu's admirer. "The Beatles will be playing here soon enough."

"I'm off to find them."

"Please do not rush away, sir," the young man said winningly. "The bands don't start playing their numbers until well after nine, so that gives you plenty of time to relax and chat with us. Please have a seat. My name is Klaus. Let's order more drinks, shall we? Do you like our German beer?"

What followed next is mostly lost to me in a drunken haze. It seems that maybe I talked about art and literature with this Klaus guy whose tastes were most decidedly beatnik. In due course I was holding the hand of a blond. At first she moved away from me when I tried to kiss her. Then she melted up and began to kiss me with interest. Soon she shifted gears to be reluctant again.

"Hey, they throw you out of the Liddypool or what, skin?" called out a Liverpudlian accent in a friendly-insulting fashion. I instantly recognized the little bloke with the beard, greased back hair and protruding nose who had called out.

"Say again, whacker," I called back.

"Remember me Yank...from the Jac, then? I'm a drummer by trade, you see, la. At least it's what I list as me trade on me tax forms. Me name is Richie Starkey, but me mates and fans, like, call me Ringo...Ringo Starr."

"Yeah, sure, I remember you. Ringo Starr! You're the guy with all the rings on your fingers."

"That's me all right," chirped Ringo, holding up his hands to proudly display his rings.

Although I barely knew Ringo Starr (I think George had introduced us in the toilet at the Jac where we had all by chance descended upon it at the same time) I shook hands with him as though he was a long lost brother of mine.

"You're playing here tonight, skin?"

"Rory, the lads and meself will go up on stage in a few more ticks, whacker. Sticking around for the hoe-down, mate?"

"Yeah, I'll be here for a while, but I'm really hunting for Lennon and his lot, skin."

It delighted me to use and to be referred to as 'skin', as it made me feel like I belonged, and it only seemed natural to call this likeable tiny drummer 'skin', 'whacker', or 'mate'...all meaning 'friend' in Scouse.

"They're over at the Indra, them. Ah, awful place it is, really. The lads hate the gig to death, like it's the truth, I know it. But its' good practice for them at least, I think. You have to pay your dues if you want to sing the blues."

"How's the new drummer working out for the Beatles? Let's see, I can't remember the guy's name."

"That'll be Pete Best. He's a trooper like meself. Nothing fancy but he keeps the soldiers marching. None of that jazzy crap, just hard beating rock n roll. He puts in his hard day's night like meself."

"I'm dying to see the lads."

"During me first break I'll run you over there, then."

The music began and I quickly found myself using dance

steps I had never seen before with a fraulien with an enormous set of breasts. I was living right.

A quick comment from Rory Storm and the Hurricanes, "In many ways they were a primitive forerunner of glitter rock. Their stage show sparkled and hopped with lightening." The athletic Rory, with his flips and jumps, is by far the most energetic rocker Liverpool his probably ever produced, including Elvis Costello and the Pet Shop Boys. It is only a quirk of fate that Rory was completely bypassed when the British Invasion was launched upon the shores of America from England. I'm not sure if Rory Storm and the Hurricanes ever even cut a record, but if they didn't it was America's loss.

Ringo was as good as his word, herding me over to the Indra, which was less than a five minute walk from the Kaiserskellar. By that time I was pissed out of my head and floating on air. We entered the Indra to be greeted by loud music and a rough-looking crowd that was apparently dividing its attention between the raw music on the stage and a fist fight on the dance floor. The combat was between two drunk men who were wearing different types of seaman outfits. I took one of the sailors to be a Swede or Norwegian. He was a big brute of a man who was slow with his fists but who was able to connect with great power whenever one of his blows landed. The other naval chap, who was small and thin, appeared to be either an Italian or a Frenchman. The little man was fast and scrappy, but he lacked any real strength behind his punches.

The fight ended when the Nordic landed a clean and straight right hook on the Latin's jaw. The crowd responded with loud applause at the spectacle. The Northern victor was, however, awarded for his K.O. by being stormed by a half a dozen of stocky German bouncers. The Nordic, still fighting mad, broke loose from the bouncers and kicked the downed Latin in the groin.

"That isn't cricket, mate!" Ringo called out in protest.

"That's a low blow!" I yelled. "Foul! Foul!"

The bouncers, who had perhaps learned their tactics from the vicious Storm troopers of the Second World War, proceeded to massacre the big Swede with all varieties of punches and kicks. In a few moments the huge fellow was on the floor lying unconscious next to the fallen Italian who, though still battered and dazed, took the opportunity to spit in his face.

"Seig heil, mein herr!" Lennon shouted out over the microphone. "I see my good friend Mr. Al Capone-Moran from the Arty Farty School in Giddy Liddypool via Chi-Fly Town of Yankee-doodle Dandy land is out there in the audience. Please leave those corpses there and approach the stage with the engaging Mr. Starr."

"Hey, Al, up here!" shouted Paul.

"Hello, Dr. Moran," added George.

"Good to see you sir, professor!" threw in Stu, trying to get in on the act.

"Welcome to Krautland!" hollered John.

I was dismayed at the way the lads just abruptly stopped their performances to shout me their greeting. It didn't seem very professional to me and it was embarrassing. I waved back to them before waving down a waiter and ordering a drink.

"What about a drink, mate?" I asked Ringo, adding, "I'm buying."

"I'll only have a quick one, whacker. I have to earn me living like any other working la' from the Dingle," said Ringo.

Meanwhile, the Beatles, unconcerned by the annoyed responses of their audience, unstrapped their guitars and took an impromptu break to greet me. With good natured jollity they patted my back and shook my hand, hustling me off to a table.

"Here now, Ringo, don't you have a job to be off to then?" joked Pete Best, the Beatles' latest addition. This young man was a remarkably good looking fellow with dark hair, swarthy complexion and handsome features. He also had a good build and an athletic air about him. Without a doubt this Pete Best was the best looking, as well as the best shaped of the lot. He was a marked contrast to John, Paul, George and Stu, with their rather thin, puny and boyish bodies.

"Aye, I'm off in one mo, Mr. Best," replied Ringo. "We start a wee bit earlier than you, so I'm already on my first intermission."

"I see, la," Pete said rather coolly.

"Not to worry any, Pete," snorted Paul in his best John-like manner. "Ringo here isn't interested in your bloody job."

"Why would he want to leave Rory for the likes of us, eh? You're safe, Pete son," counter-jabbed John, in his nasty, needling fashion.

"He can have this bleeding job if he'll swap me his posh job with the Hurricanes," Pete responded in a hard guy voice. Unlike most people this Peter Best wasn't in the least bit fazed by John and Paul's verbal attacks.

"Sensitive Pete is," laughed Paul, ignoring Pete to grasp my hand. "You're a sight for sore eyes, Al. It's happy we are to see you, a mate from home and all."

"How was your trip over, Dr. Moran?" Stu asked politely.

My answer was lost among the good cheer and the noises we were all making. I was absolutely delighted to be with the lads again. But I must admit that their general appearance put me off somewhat. In the past although they were always poorly dressed they had normally been well-groomed, whereas now all their overall looks had declined since their departure from home. They were even scruffier than their scruffiest days at the Jac. Only Paul and Pete seemed to have any interest in personal hygiene, while Lennon positively stank, his hair glistening with grease and his face glowing with oily sweat. All of the boys were physically rundown, their faces creased with nightlife wrinkles. Underfed and underweight, their hyperactive behavior belied their physical realities. Lennon in particular was like a comet racing across the night sky, literally sparkling with a high strung giddy energy.

"We were afraid you'd not show, Al!" shouted Lennon before giving a beer a draining in a few gulps.

"How is the Arty and all that, then?" asked John.

"It is the same as ever."

"And how is Ginny Jenny Henny Penny Boone Boomer Brownee Browne?" roared John. "I mean, like your old flame! Is she your wife yet? Ho ho ho, ha!"

"No, she isn't, John, She did see me off at the Lime."

"Go on now brown cow!"

"But she's not really interested in me."

"She really got a hold on you, skin. Not to worry, that. I have a pretty German fraulein for your old salty soul."

Ringo took off and the Beatles wandered back up to the stage. The music started up again after much shouting from the audience and bouncers. Even in my sodden condition I could hear that their musical style sounded better than before. It had become more polished. For all their hyper energy and continued clowning and swearing, the Beatles were honing their skills and graduating from playing Liverpool church basement dances and sleazy strip joints to becoming a professional nightclub act. I recognized several new tunes, one that I imagined that Lennon and McCartney had written intermittently together. Pete Best on the drums was a vast improvement over what had gone on before. He gave the group a consistently steady backbeat.

However, it was obvious that both Paul and George had made tremendous leaps forward to becoming a tight bass lead. Stu, who was also playing bass, was virtually soundless, adding nothing to the group's standard except as a James Dean décor. John too, didn't contribute much with his guitar playing, but his raw voice more than made up for his lack of instrumental activity.

I got drunker and drunker and then sicker and sicker. I blacked out and had to be dragged back home by the Beatles at closing time.

I awoke to find myself sandwiched in between John and George in a too-small foldout bed. We all stank to high heaven. Our feet stuck out at the foot of the bed. In the distance a Hamburg church bell announce the arrival of Sunday mass. I closed my eyes and tried to blot out the throb in my head. My stomach hurt from throwing up. I was happy.

CHAPTER TEN

It was sometime around noontime when the lads began to wake up and move about. One by one they wearily pulled themselves out of bed and slipped on their dirty clothes without the benefit of bathing. Everybody was hung over and a bit sick to the stomach with me being in the worst condition. Lennon wasn't far behind me.

"Fancy some breakfast, Al?" asked Lennon, his lips smiling with false sweetness in an effort at bravado.

"Yuk! Don't make me sick again, John," I mumbled, although I felt a grim satisfaction that I wasn't the only jerk suffering from a king size hangover.

"Some cornflakes will do you good, son," said John.

"We're having cornflakes for breakfast! You gotta be shitting me, man."

"No, son, I'm not shitting you. Cornflakes is our standard bill of fare here."

"It's all the likes of us can afford to buy," George said seriously, his long face twisting into a look of distaste. "Sunday mornings always meant a big breakfast to at me house in Speke. Me mum was at her best in the kitchen that morning of the week."

"I did the cooking at our place," Paul cut in, his voice thick with reflection. "Usually we had muffins smothered in marmalade with a pile of bacon to the side. Me Da was generous with the larder on Sundays, he was."

"We ain't home then, are we children?" John sharply butted in with that tone of voice that indicated he was hurting the most.

"Only talking Johnny," Paul said softly.

"Only talking, what? You fellas may as well cut the

Dylan Thomas poetry recital about the bountiful breakfast tables at home because none of that will come true here, I'm thinking," snorted John.

"Bloody cornflakes," grumbled George.

"All that trouble we went through to come to bloody Germany just to starve to death," pitched in Stu.

"The bloody prisoners of war had it better in the German concentration camps than we do," added Pete.

The bitching session appeared to be blossoming into a full scale rebellion when I decided to help Lennon quell it for the time being.

"You guys may be poor working musicians but I'm a tourist here on vacation in Germany to toss my money around as I please."

"Good for you, Moran," Lennon said without humor.

"And this morning I want to toss a bundle on the biggest breakfast Hamburg can scare up for six hungry guys from Liverpool," I announced, feeling like Santa Claus.

My gesture was rewarded with delighted whoops.

"You're a regular St. Nick, Al," declared Paul.

With that the five Beatles and I marched off to find a friendly German restaurant where we ordered eggs, bacon, toast, sausage, marmalade, coffee and orange juice among other things. To tease George I ordered him a bowl of cornflakes. Once again I was treated to the sight of the Beatles tearing away at their food. Lennon, behaving like a famished cannibal, gobbled down more than the rest, devouring three full plates of food before the vicious glow inside of his eyes began to diminish. In a study of contrast to the gluttonous Beatles, I nursed a cup of coffee and a glass of orange juice.

"Eat some there, Al, it will settle your stomach, I'm thinking," counseled George.

I took Harrison's advice and managed to choke down and

keep down some toast and bacon. George's wisdom was sound and I began to feel better instantly.

"Any plans for today, men?" I asked.

"I'm sorry, Dr. Moran," said Stu, blushing deeply. "Have a date."

"Our Stu is in love," teased John gently.

"Yes, I know," I said with a knowing smile. "I met her last night."

"What?"

"She was at the other club with some other people. One of the guys' names was Klaus. She's in love too, I think. It was plain to see. I thought she was a very beautiful woman."

Stu glowed with pleasure.

"What are you other guys doing today?" I tried my luck again.

"I'm off too, myself. So sorry Uncle Albert," said Paul, appearing ill at ease because he was ditching me after I had bought him the best breakfast he had had since arriving in Hamburg.

"Is it a girl?"

"Quite. I have a fraulein and it's like this, I can only see her in the morning before she goes off to work."

"You mean you have to shag her before her husband comes home from work, eh, Paulie?" leered John.

I was going to ask Pete what he was planning to do but he merely shrugged his shoulders and continued to eat as if to blot me out.

"Don't fret it Al, you're with cousin George and Uncle John today," announced John, putting us all back at our ease.

The day was warmish in a European sense, especially considering the season. I was feeling revived for the most part as John, George and I boarded a bus.

"Have a looksee, Dr. Moran," instructed John, rushing me to window seat. With a bit of a show off gesture Lennon immediately took the seat beside me as George dutifully took a seat behind us. He leaned forward between our heads as if to catch every word of our conversation. I, as well as George; was keenly aware that Lennon was playing the mature adult college student to George's naïve high school dropout role. I felt a bit sorry to see the way George followed the script every time. It was Liverpool all over again.

"Well, George, do you miss England?" I asked, trying to make the lad feel more of a part of the outing, as it was clear he was John's choice for 'odd man out'.

"Not at all," George said too quickly to be believable, but he also added. "But I miss Liverpool rather a lot."

"And his mummy," quipped John.

"And you don't miss your aunt or Cynthia?" asked George reproachfully.

"Not one bit, son," said John nonchalantly, playing hard guy.

"Bloody liar," George whispered in my ears.

I smiled and nodded my head, pleased to be a part of a conspiracy with George against John for change.

"Fancy a woman of your choice, Al?" Lennon asked with a wink. He had quickly caught on that I was favoring George that morning, so he was making maneuvers to lure me back with a different sort of bait. If the Hamburg sights weren't enough to win me he's offer me Hamburg sluts.

"Bit early for that chat, what?' asked George.

"Too early for me at any rate," I seconded.

"Did sweet Gin put a lock on your trousers as well, mate?" challenged John.

"Nah, it's my hangover that is keeping my trousers up."

"Does a hangover make you impotent or something?" said John shrilly, applying the pressure in that bullying way of his. "Me, the worse me bloody hangover is the higher me sex drive is. Must be the German yeast in the beer stimulating me cockles. Ho, ho, ho! What, then?"

"He only just got here, like, John," put in George, taking my side.

"Surely you have a lovely medieval cathedral or some dead baron's castle to show me. After all, I'm only a lousy American tourist here for the historical perspective of Hamburg. I even bought my cheap Japanese camera," I said, holding up my camera.

"You can take a jump into the Rhine with the guidebook stuff, Al. First we can take a walk in the Reperbohn."

"It's the red light district, Dr. Moran," explained George.

"All of that this early in the day?" I asked weakly. "Surely we won't be able to see the nice red lights at this time of day."

"They're on all day, son…this I know."

"It doesn't interest me much either," intoned George. "There's plenty of that sort working the Albert Docks at home."

"Then go home, George, if you don't like it so bloody much," barked John, turning nasty. "I only want to show him a bit of fun for the smashing breakfast he treated us to. Some of us English still have enough manners and grace to return a favor."

George sulked into silence as John had intended him to.

"Some other time, Lennon," I said tartly.

"I'll tell you what, then. I'll just take you to it to show you so you'll know where it is when you're keen on getting it on. Okay?"

"Well, I don't know."

"It's nearby, then."

"Okay, I guess."

"What about you, Harrison?"

"I'm here, aren't I, Johnny?"

We got off the bus and began to make our way to the Reperbohn, which was only a stone's throw away. The Reperbohn is like any host of other red light districts or combat zones in Western Europe or the States, with its scores of low life drinking dives, strip joints, dirty bookstores and houses of ill repute. However, perhaps the Reperbohn is the lewdly of them all. Hundreds of prostitutes, coming in all shapes, sizes, ages and races, were standing in front of rows of houses, doing their upmost to ply their trade.

My head, which had previously ached with the dogged pain of a determined hangover, began to make a stunning comeback. At the back of my burning sore bruised brain there was the start of a tingle of pleasure. Soon this feeling was starting to bubble across the raw surface of the damaged insides of my head until it spread across the rest of my body. The end result of it all was a mammoth erection. My condition reminded me of my essentially lonely existence in England. Loneliness and aloneness are probably responsible for most sexual acts in the world. Now being the furthest away that I had ever been from Chicago, my juices began to come to a boil. I was horny and I wanted a woman.

"Changing your mind, are we then, Al?" guffawed Lennon, nodding his head towards my obvious excitement.

"Piss off, Lennon!"

"No need to be ashamed, mate, I'm there with you," said John sincerely, unbuttoning his black leather jacket to reveal his similar state.

"Maybe you're right about a hangover on German beer increasing one's sex drive after all."

"No need to sound like Sigmund Freud about it, Al. We're only dying to plunge into the blond bush of some German wench. Am I right, skin, wot?"

George looked at the two of us in that mournful air of his, looking grieved by Rabbias commentary. It was wrong of us to speak so openly in front of a boy at the age where he's still sorting out his own sexuality. I was ashamed to think that George wasn't even seventeen yet.

"I think I'll mosey on down the road by meself, mates," broadcasted George, putting down his head and peculiar heading towards the bus stop.

"See you, George," I called out feebly.

"See you, la," he called behind himself.

"Don't let the birds scare you off when your bird can sing, young fella," hooted John.

"No birds scare me, Lennon."

"Come on back, then, and get some practice at shagging. It will put you in good stead with the colleens back home, not to mention the happiness it will bring to the future Mrs. Harrison," taunted John, once again exhibiting a peculiar pleasure in the discomfort of another person. It was an awful aspect of an otherwise unique character.

"Lennon, you go too far. Hell, he's only a boy yet. It's simply terrible how you put him through the ringer like this. You try to control him and the others too much," I said low enough so George couldn't hear my words. I didn't want him to think I was patronizing him.

"Don't waste your Catholic tears and fears on our George, Al, because he's doing okay by himself with plenty of girlies, birds and frauleins. They love the innocent, don't you know?"

"Maybe he isn't keen on whores like you."

"One could argue that all women are basically whores?"

"One would have to be a real asshole to think that. You know better to talk like this and I can't believe you think that way…not for one minute. You have it in you to be a real shit. Think of Cynthia, Aunt Mimi, Paul's mum, my mother, Mrs.

Harrison and your own mummy."

"Sorry, mate, these German beer hangovers are making us both rather quarrelsome. I retract me statement in honor of Mrs. Harrison, she's gear."

"Okay, let's drop it, then," I agreed, but got in the last word on the topic with: "Besides, most women are gear."

"Yeah, man," agreed John. "A quick rock n roll and rump will soon put us straight. Afterwards we'll be able to drink and laugh together again like old buddies, eh? I'm glad to see you again mate, really."

"And it's good to see you as well. I missed you all but mostly I missed you. Liverpool is bland without your band."

In this tender moment it was difficult to know who the real John Lennon was. I'm sure that other people felt as I did.

"I'm sorry about taking the piss out of George like that. Honestly, he's more of a man of than you imagine. Now let's stop all this short temper business and get to our long trumpet business. It's time to blow, to bebop, toot, toot, shoot, shoot, shoot. I'm as hard as Chinese geometry, mate."

"I guess I'll go along for the ride."

"Spot us the admission price and later I'll find you a woman who will attach no price to her kisses. In fact, I'll repay you in full at the club tonight."

I lent John a handful of marks and allowed myself to be captured by a blond bombshell with breasts the size of the Liverpool stripper John had once set me up with the moment we stepped into one of the houses.

"Yours reminds me of thousands of chesty chestnuts I've seen in a thousand dirty magazines," John chuckled into my ear as he patted me on the back.

"Now it's your turn, John."

"And here's my turn just now."

To my utter amazement John selected a rather short, fat, dark-haired non Germanic looking woman, one that could only inspire lust in a blind man or a drunken sailor on shore leave after a five month duty at sea. Looking at the woman again, I changed the five months to five years. To be point blank, she was ugly as sin.

"Want to borrow my glasses Lennon? You're going blind?" I giggled as we climbed the stairwell.

"Let's make the poor thing happy, eh? Share the wealth, what?" John said with bravado, giving me a silly harsh look as he took the plump gal's hand and let her steer him into a room.

"Suit yourself, John."

"Besides, I had your bird last week."

"You're a regular wise guy!"

"That I shall always remain, whacker."

The door closed behind Lennon.

"Who needs Liverpool?" I said to my escort.

Lennon suddenly reopened the door and called after me: "Shall the two of us join you two?"

There was no mirth in his question.

"You're not serious, are you?"

"Why not mate? A foursome would be a lark. One bed, like. It would be nice, Al. Very sharing and Marxist and all that sort of rubbish. Wot's that, then?"

"Another time," I said not really going for the idea.

In spite of my negative feelings 'the another time' happened sooner than I had ever anticipated.

True to his word, Lennon introduced me to several women that very night. These female ranged from the beautiful to the dreadful. At various times he introduced me as an art professor; at other times he introduced me as an American beatnik poet; at still other times he merely said, 'he's a fucking

Yank tourist". Oddly enough, more than a few times he referred to me as the manager of the Beatles, who was currently searching of a New York record company to produce the groups' first LP.

I took his introductions as a gag but one time he raised my ire by saying, 'Hey, luv, say 'howdy' to this New York tourist' he's here to blow his 'wad' of money as well as his wad of..."

"Lennon!"

"Sorry, lover, I was just kidding. He's really Paul's bloody Uncle Albert from Nottingham."

After many tankards of German Beer and the attention of some women, my hangover magically disappeared, as if the fresh liquor had washed away the damaged and battered brain cells.

"I want more beer!" I shouted, working on a new hangover.

Although the Beatles usually had Sundays off, they had run up an excessively high bar bill, thus they were playing to pay off their debt. The five of them looked vicious in their black leather jackets and rumbled clothing. The stage lights gave them a sinister surrealistic Elvis jailhouse rock image. The music was unnecessarily loud that night, but their voices were mixing in all sorts of strange harmonics that made our doo whoop street corner singers back home sound like choirboys. Paul, George and Pete were all doing a good job of coordinating their musical sound in a tight bass-lead drums combo; maybe the first power trio. They sounded good. Lennon was at his howling and snarling rebellious working class hero best, maybe even out-Elvising Elvis at his best early honky-tonk days.

"You're on the money tonight," I shouted at John over the din at an intermission.

"It's the beer talking, Al," laughed John, pleased in spite of himself.

"Then we'll have to take plenty of beer back to Liverpool with us if that's what it'll take to make everybody love your music."

"Maybe we'll never make it back to Liverpool," he said wistfully.

It was the first sign he had betrayed of being homesick. Before this he had been unwilling to freely show that he missed home like the others. It was the first time on my trip that John briefly came out from behind his giddy rocker persona and revealed himself to be a young scouser on his own faraway.

As the night progressed the crowd became rowdier and noisier. The dingy beer cellar filled up with a pungent smell of beer, sweat, joy and sex. That night it was the most wonderful place in the world. I forgot my age and status to allow myself to let a pretty blond rub her body against mine in a lewd dance. We weren't alone. The music grew louder and louder. A strange yet intense sexuality sprayed the hall with its own exotic aroma. I, a rapidly aging man, found myself dancing with a throbbing erection. My partner laughed and treasured the moment. I felt her stroking hand reaching towards my crotch whenever the packed crowd crushed us together. Then her body began to stroke me up and down across my body, with an emphasis upon my groin area. She was well-practiced at this sort of ballet, I thought, using her body to whip pleasure over me.

"Very well-practiced," I spat out as my brain almost melted with pleasure and my soul was elevated up to the stars from the shocked intensity of my dance hall orgasm. It was only the beginning.

I was gulping my beer now, believing I had the capacity of a decadent Roman emperor.

"Lennon, you ole sot and sot, you got me drunk again," I slobbered, spitting beer on his jacket as I grabbed him in a bear hug.

"Steady, Yank," scolded Lennon, freezing his face hard.

"Sorry, mate," I said, backing off. "I just have had too much wine, women and dong for my old tourist soul."

"Dong, you say?"

"Yeah, dong…you know, cock, penis."

"Oh great, dong!" he cackled, returning my hug. "Wine, women and dong, that's you and me both, old son."

"Hooray for Liverpool!"

"And Chicago!"

"And Hamburg!"

Some Germans lifted their mugs in salute.

Paul came by holding the hand of a pretty fraulein.

"Being naughty, are we Dr. Moran?" he asked with a grin.

"Hooray for the Irish of Chicago and Liverpool!" I declared, clapping McCartney on the back.

"Our dear professor is being a right rowdy old pervert tonight," professed John, goosing me.

"Give him some bennies, Johnny. We're all in for a long night ahead of us, I reckon," said Paul.

Lennon encircled my waist with his arms and whispered into my ear, "Fancy some pills to help you through the night, Al? Pills for thrills, eh?"

"What sort of pills? I am not sick."

"Like candy, la," said John slyly. "Aye, Dr. Lennon personally prescribes them for you, even if you aren't sick."

"Wot's this then, Uncle Albert?" said Paul, stunned. "Are we interested in such lowly things, then?"

"If your pills are illegal I'm not interested."

"Isn't beer illegal back in Chicago?" questioned John. "I have heard about Prohibition or something, Al Capone and all that rot."

"Where were you during the St. Valentine's Day Massacre?" teased Paul.

"And I thought all you beatniks were into smoking tea and shooting heroin," challenged John.

"I'll tell you and the whole cockeyed world I didn't do any of those things. I'm a drinker and that's plenty enough to worry about."

"You ever do horse?" Paul shouted too loudly.

"Let's not inform the whole bloody world, Paulie."

"Did you ever read that famous book about drug addicts by one of those famous Beatniks writer fellers?" asked Paul, blowing off John.

"Do you mean Jack Kerouac's *On the Road*?"

"That's not the one I'm on about. I'm on about *Naked Lunch* by William Burroughs. Maybe it was banned in the States but we got a hold of it in England and we all thought it was gear at the Inny," said Paul.

"I didn't realize you're a reader, McCartney."

"Yes, I am indeed a reader, Dr. Moran," retorted Paul. "And I'm now reading *Packed Lunch* by I.B. Greedy."

It was standard Beatle cheek: always quick on the comeback. Against my better judgment I took the pills John offered me and stuffed them into my mouth. I washed them down with beer. From the point onward the night spilled forward, ending in a drunken blur back in the double bed above the club.

The night is now blurry in my mind beyond all recall. It seems to me that at one point I was in a body crowded with naked people and we were all having a pretty good time. I can't swear to who did what to whom!

The bed gradually began to empty as the dawn's early rays began to sweep across the dusty attic floor. Unable to sleep, my sleepy-silly whimsy recalled the scene in the old 1920s German silent vampire movie, *Nosferatu,* where Count Orlock (nee Dracula) was destroyed by a ray of light streaking through the bedroom window of his last victim. The monster had lingered too long over a delicious female throat and thus vanished when the morning arrived and found him out of his coffin. The dying heroine's arms had taken away the Count's will to outrun the sun. I thought of this long-forgotten movie as I received a final blow job. John, by my side, watched with a bored look on his face.

"I'm in heaven," I sighed.

"German beer makes a bloke horny," remarked John.

George, lying on the other side of the bed, snored softly. Then I felt dirty and sad.

"Bloody Hamburg is rainier than Liverpool," grumbled George Harrison, clamping his lips around a cigarette. The smoke he puffed out joined that of the other four Beatles. I wasn't a smoker so that freed up my hand to clutch my suitcase.

"I'm rather anxious to get back," I said to no one in particular.

"Where's the bloody train?" mumbled Pete Best. "I thought that the bloody Germans were supposed to be so bloody efficient with their train schedules."

The others looked back at Pete with apparent dismay, for only he appeared eager to see me off. For my part I didn't feel any fondness for this strange lad. He was certainly a fine drummer who had provided the glue to stick together the band's sound. And this Pete Best had certainly never been or offensive. On the other hand, not one single time during my entire visit did he ever make an attempt to warm up to me. I don't recall one simple question directed towards me by him. He appeared determined to ignore my presence altogether. I can only put it down to that he had never known me back in Liverpool, thus I wasn't his friend at all. I was only John, Paul, George and Stu's mate. I felt put out by Pete's attitude because I'm a rather typical American in that I flatter myself that all people will warm up to me given time. Then too, I guess it's the competitive spirit of young men of the world to put 'my friend' and 'your friend' labels on people and he was reluctant to muscle in on John and the others. I just wasn't part of Pete Best's world.

"Anxious to get back to the Arty, are you?" asked Stu, a wistful look coming into his eyes. He wasn't fooling anybody with his rocker act, least of all himself. His path was beckoning him back to the art world and away from Lennon and the Beatles. We all knew that it was a matter of time. In my heart, I hoped Stu's German girlfriend would be the one to unlock the chain that bound him to the others.

"Want to come back with me, Stu, lad?" I only half jested.

"Wot's that, then?" giggled Stu, sounding like John.

"Your place is back in college and not here," I continued in a semi-serious manner. "We all know that."

"He doesn't want to be a lousy art professor like some other failed artists we can all mention by first name…Al, so don't be putting any foolish notions inside of the lad's head," Lennon said cruelly to put me in my place as an outsider and to maintain the closed ranks of his troops.

"He'd be better off being a failed artist than a failed bassist," Paul said thoughtfully. "Leastways, nobody would have to hear his rubbish."

"I'm a failed artist but Stu is too talented to follow in my footsteps, Mr. McCartney," I said to Paul but shooting a rueful look at Lennon.

"Failed artist or not I bloody well should be the only bassist in the band," insisted Paul.

"You're the only person here who appreciates what I can do with a brush," said Stu gratefully, ignoring Paul.

"It has to be a bloody improvement over what you can do with a guitar pick in your hands," whined Paul.

Even in those days Paul was generally the sweetest natured of the Beatles, but he could get nasty in his dealings whenever he wanted something. However, I put Paul's behavior down to juvenile rivalry than any true meanness of spirit on Paul's part.

"Stu is a Beatle like the rest of us," barked John.

"He'll be a failed Beatle before it's finished," I shot back with assurance.

Before any more words could be exchanged Paul blurted out, "Heil Hitler! Wot's this then? Is it the train? Mother Mary come to me, it's on time right enough. Heil Germany!"

At least compared to Pete Best's quietness and aloofness, Paul McCartney was almost always cheerful and talkative. I suspected he was eager to see me off so he could see another one of his numerous girlfriends.

"You got everything then, Al?" worried George, shaking my hand. Over the extended weekend my feelings for Harrison had grown warmer. We had somehow put together a pact of friendship during my short stay.

"And you'll look in on our gaffers and mummies and aunties and such and tell 'em we're still as sweet as apple tarts or jam butties and keeping well and fine?" chirped Paul, pumping my hand in the glad hand Chicago Irish politician fashion of his. Mayor Daley's machine could have put Paul to good use in Chicago's River Wards.

"So long," mumbled Pete, sharing a stronger handshake than I thought him capable of. "Tell Liverpool to get ready for the Beatles. We're getting honed up just now and we'll be home directly."

"Your drumming has been a great improvement for the group Pete."

"Thank you, mate."

Maybe this Pete Best was a good guy after all. I would never find out as this was perhaps the last time I ever saw him except for a chance encounter on a Liverpool street several years later. He recognized me I'm sure, but he walked past without saying anything.

"Tell the fellers at the Arty to study hard and not to sniff too much paint remover or they'll be tossed out like Lennon," laughed Stu, gently shaking my hand and then roughly punching my arm.

Then it was Lennon's turn, "Bloody rain."

"Yeah, bloody rain."

"So it's back to Gin and the pubs, is it?"

"I suppose so. Life is long and needs to be spent somehow."

"Bloody rain," repeated Lennon, looking up into the dark, weeping sky. It wasn't in him to say anything nice in a parting.

CHAPTER ELEVEN

On my return to England I picked up my life from where I had left off as an instructor at the Liverpool College of Art. I also once again resumed my luckless pursuit of Ginny Browne who was now a last year student.

Once again I lost track of the Beatles. I wrote a few letters to Lennon, but apparently his rock n roll lifestyle ruled out his writing back to a former teacher. Coupled with the lack of correspondence with John, I also lost touch with the thriving Mersey Beat scene as I took to avoiding the Liverpool pop art lifestyle. I preferred the quieter, darker pubs that catered to the middle-aged and lonely.

The autumn term quickly rolled away into the annuals as I added an extra roll of fat around my belly and lost more than a few strands of hair.

In my loneliness, I sought out ways to pass time away from my teaching duties. I started a notebook of drawings of Liverpool scenes. My favorite settings were the Custom House and the ferryboats that worked the Mersey River. I also included a couple of drawings of my favorite students, one of these being the beautiful Cynthia Powell. In the future I would mail the drawing to Mrs. Lennon during the terrible period following her divorce from Mr. Lennon. I have no way of knowing if she ever received it. However, that is jumping ahead of the story by seven or eight years.

My collection also included a rather professional etching of Gerry Marsden, who had been an enjoyable student of mine before he suffered the same fate as Lennon and lost his student grant and was sent down from the college.

"Now I'll have to earn me keep as a rock n roller or as a postman or me Mum will toss me out of the house. Ha, me a post mail," cracked Gerry, in typical scouse bravado, as he took his leave of the college. After leaving the college Gerry went back over to Hamburg with his band the Pacemakers to work the same club circuit as the Beatles. Somebody told me that Gerry had gained and lost a postal route in less than a month's time.

I had asked Gin to sit for me but she always had better things to do and she told me so. I wondered if she wanted no part of me because she knew I had no ability as an artist, whereas she had more than enough elbow grease to garnish a living with her pencils and brushes. Was she only snubbing a lowly teacher?

For some unaccountable reason I took my pen and began to write fiction and poetry for the first time in my life. I suppose I wrote to pass the time, but I also began to imagine myself as a Conan Doyle figure who as a young medical doctor, turned to writing as a means of supplementing his paltry income. My creative energies had always been put to use in the areas of visual arts…drawing and painting…but now I was attempting to express myself on paper. In a way, Lennon's literary efforts had encouraged me to try my own hand at it as well.

To my surprise and delight, I had an immediate success with a short story written in the horror fiction genre that was snapped up by a London magazine that paid me the princely fee of five pounds. The money covered several weeks of pub crawling. The current popularity of Hammer Productions, featuring Christopher Lee and Peter Cushing, had led to an increase interest in the macabre. Unfortunately, my next few scary tales fruitlessly made the rounds of all the available magazines before winding up in my dresser drawer. To save my ego, I managed to place a couple of poems before that market dried up as well. My writing career soon lapsed into silence. I started and abandoned a novel in a week's span.

"I guess I'm no writer, either," I began to say to myself, wondering if my literary career would end up being marooned like my painting career.

However, I began to reason that writing unsuccessful pieces was more productive than doing nothing at all. My Catholic schoolboy guilt was able to overrule my writer's block and I was back on a set schedule of typing.

I finally settled upon the idea of writing a book about Nathaniel Hawthorne, the American author of *The Scarlet Letter*, who had spent a few years in Liverpool working for the U.S. Embassy. Hawthorne was a rather dour and brooding Puritanical man given to a dark world view which provided me with a source of comfort in those dismal days of my life. The book soon shrunk into an essay that only focused upon Hawthorne's day of England. Eventually this single essay would serve as a stepping stone to a series of short essays concerning the exploits of American expatriates who lived in England for a time, such as Stephen Crane, T.S. Elliot, Henry James and so on. I wasn't unhappy when I wrote the pieces and I also wasn't unhappy when the collection was accepted by both English and American publishing houses.

It was the Friday just before the Christmas holidays began and I was penciling in the last of my student's grades when there came a light rap upon my office door.

"Please come in," I called out, a bit annoyed to be disturbed at such a time. I hoped it wasn't a grade complainer.

The door opened and Ginny Browne popped her head in through the door. "May I come in to see you, Dr. Moran?"

"Yes, come in please, Miss Browne."

Closing the door behind her, Gin took the chair next to my desk. "I'm glad I caught you before you left on holiday."

"I'm still here but I'm considering going to Scotland for the break."

"Scotland is marvelous but it's so cold this time of year. The place is so cold and wet. Then again, I imagine all of Britain is cold and wet at this time of the year. But why don't you go back home?"

"I can always see Chicago when I return to the States, so I

figure I'll spend my time and money seeing the British Isles before going back."

"That makes sense," she remarked, seemingly lost in thought. I could sense that she was nervous and that she wasn't comfortable being with me. Keep it official, I warned myself.

"So what's on your mind, Miss Browne?"

"It's like this, sir…Al, I mean," she began slowly. "I want to apply for admission into a graduate course in the U.S."

"So you're going for your Masters of Arts?" I asked with pleasure. "It's a good idea."

"Yes, I think it's my best bet to so. Do you think I'm able to do it?"

"Sure you can. I don't see any reason why not. Heck, you were always one of my top students."

She lost her awkwardness long enough to beam a smile at me. "I want to study at the University of Wisconsin."

"That's in Madison, not far from Chicago. It's a great school. I know for certain. But Madison, Wisconsin is incredibly cold during the winter. The winters up there make your English winters seem tropical. Say, my mother was originally from that state. Some godforsaken village called Kenosha. Wisconsin is just due north of my state of Illinois." I was babbling, making talk. I wanted to keep her as long as possible. She nodded eagerly as I spoke, not really listening to my gushing.

"Perhaps you'll do me a favor then. A wee one it is."

"I'll do anything within reason."

"I need several references and I was wondering if I could trouble you, Dr. Moran. After all, you have been my instructor in one or two classes and you would be as good of a judge of my abilities as anybody," she said in a formal style, her face frozen in a hard smile.

"I'd be delighted to help you." I said after deciding not to make her sweat it out. Besides I was professional enough not to want to take advantage of my situation.

"It's only a tiny form to fill out."

"You're an excellent student who will merit a scholarship."

"That's grand of you to say Al, but have you forgotten my first name?"

We shared a gentle laugh before I shifted gears.

"I will write you a reference on the first request but you've refused my request to sit for me dozens of times this past term. All of my other favorite students have sat for me, including Mr. Marsden and Miss Powell. It's the Chicago way where one favor warrants another favor."

"And it's the Liverpool way as well, luv? Can I still accommodate you on the drawing thing, Al, or did I kick away my chance forever."

"It's never too late for me."

"You know, I have been frightfully busy this term. And you have a bad habit of asking me to sit whenever I'm too busy. I'm sorry if you took it the wrong way. No need to get your nose out of joint so easily. I never intended to hurt you."

"Are you available sometime next week?"

"It's so awfully close to Christmas, isn't it? I have to contend with shopping, family and that loathsome sort of traditional rubbish. Well, you know how it is, don't you?"

"It sounds like yet another brushoff."

"Don't carry on so, Al, really. And that crybaby voice you always use drives me utterly wild. You're so sulky at times and to think you're a grown man, and a college professor at that. I don't know whether to laugh in your face or slap your face."

"What does being a grown man have to do with being hurt when somebody gives you the cold shoulder after you helped them?"

"Oh, put a lid on it, mate," she laughed. "Besides, I've only just now remembered that I'm free this coming Monday. But I expect to be fed."

"It's a deal, McNeal. And I'll even throw in a pub to seal the agreement."

Concluding our bargain with a handshake, Gin gathered up her books and left my office with a smile upon her lips. A moment later a rap came again at the door and she popped her head back into my office.

"Did you know the lads are back in town?"

"What lads are you speaking of?"

"You know: Lennon and his lot of freeloaders."

"The Beatles are back in Liverpool?" I asked with growing excitement. "Are they playing anywhere nowadays?"

"They're playing at some dank and dingy little basement jazz club over on Matthew Street. It's a real Beatnik paradise. Do you know Roy McFall? No? Well, he's the owner of the joint. It's called the Cavern."

"I hadn't heard they were back. I don't go out much lately."

"Aye, they're back. They got themselves booted out of Hamburg because George was too young to qualify for a German work permit. It also seems that they had a run in with the police concerning a fire."

"Is Lennon a firebug and burning down convents?" I asked ironically but not putting anything past John.

"It is nothing sensational really. Just a tossed ciggie in a trash can. It was nothing the fire department couldn't put out inside of five minutes. It was just some such minor nonsense that the police took exception to in order to exert their authority. Bobbies are all alike. Well, I'm off. Ta."

The Cavern Club later went on to achieve international fame for being the spawning ground of the Beatles, Gerry and the

Pacemakers and several other Liverpool bands. Regardless of its notoriety, the place never set well with me. Gin had been dead accurate in describing it as a dank and dingy basement. The very air of the club reeked of a very unclean cellar with busted sewer pipes. The smell of human sweat randomly mixed with the odors of cheap perfume and boiling soup that merged into a pungent haze that bombarded one's nose the moment you entered the door.

That wasn't the worst of it.

The amps were turned up much too high, almost creating a volcanic rumbling sound that rattled the very foundations of the old building. The dance floor was always thronged with a mass of swaying bodies trying to find a few minutes of rock n roll bliss before getting back on their buses to the foundry, shop or office.

In those days the Cavern's biggest audience was drawn there by noontime music and dancing, thus the vast majority of the young people were there for a few minutes a day to help them deal with the boring routine of their lives.

Yes, the Cavern always rather depressed me. Nonetheless, the dismal surroundings, along with the German recreated Beatles did create some sort of undeniable magic that even an old codger like myself could feel and react to.

A large sign read *The Fabulous Beatles Are Back!* was hung up across the stage where five young men still clad in black leather jackets, tattered jeans and dirty tennis shoes, were turning on the audience with their newly found power source which bore little resemblance to the shaky tunes they produced before they were exiled to Hamburg.

I tried to get closer to the stage so I could wave at them. I was eager to let them know I was still interested in their careers. How quickly we are to leap upon any bandwagon heading towards the stars. My hand waved along with dozens of other sweaty palms. I was one of many.

I was gulping down the last of my Coke when a pretty

young woman came up to me and shouted into my ear, "Excuse me sir, but Mr. Lennon would like me to guide you over to his office next door."

"Lennon has an office?"

As we spoke the Beatles finished their number and Lennon gave me a wink as he unstrapped his guitar. Or so I thought he was directing the wink towards me.

"This way sir," said the girl, taking me by the hand and leading me next door to the Graper, a typical Liverpool pub, where Lennon, accompanied by another pretty young woman, was sitting at the bar and draining a pint of bitter.

"Hey, you, Dr. Moran, I'm surprised to see the likes of yourself in the likes of the Cavern," Lennon piped over his pint in that sarcastic tone of voice that was usually forthcoming of a long string of nasty tirades.

"Bugger off, rocky and roller coaster, cocky and diddly squat. And how do you do wah do?" I quipped, turning away to wave down a pint for myself. I was hoping to fend him off if he was going to act shitty.

Lennon smiled and turned back to his pint and his date. My escort, evidently unused to Lennon's harsh greetings, began to turn a flustered red.

"Stealing me lines, the auld one is," I heard Lennon grumble.

"Have you known John for long?" the girl whispered to me.

"Ages," I replied, beginning to feel uneasy myself.

"He's me auld proffy woffy from the artsy fartsy," Lennon called out, never missing a beat in his conversation with his new female interest.

"So you're a real college professor," chirped my escort, trying hard to make up for Lennon's coldness by being overly attentive.

"Careful there, luv," intoned Lennon, putting his hands on my shoulders.

"What's up, John?" I asked coolly, shaking off John's hands.

"Me old arty prof can't be wasting his time with the likes of you, a mere typing poor girl from North John Street. A man who's written books can't be larking about with a shop girl. The professor is in love with a real angel. Isn't that right, Dr. Moran?"

The girl, who had been looking more bewildered all the time, now twisted her blushing face into a crestfallen expression. I think Lennon somehow had hurt her feelings in an attempt to hurt mine. Perhaps he was trying to hurt both of our feelings.

"You go too far, Lennon," I lashed out.

"Well, aren't you in love with Ginny Browne, Yank?" John kept at it with determined viciousness.

"Never you mind about that, son, and introduce me to these lovely lasses so I can order another round for the four of us," I said, changing my tactics. I never became an expert on how to deal with John Lennon when he was being difficult.

"A round of pints earns you two names right enough mate," said John, starting to thaw a bit. "Leslie Quick by your side and make it quick with the pint to my side, for I'll fetch a switch if I miss the next lick. And this young fetching stick by me side but not me best side or back side is a trick from St. Nick with a swell kick by the name of Sandy Hicks. Sandy's maybe randy and your Leslie Quick maybe will mix. Bartender how's 'bout some cocktail mix. A stick in times saves mine," rambled John, like an inmate as a nuthouse.

"How clever you are," cooed Sandy.

"Yes he is," seconded Leslie.

I thought not but kept my peace. At that moment I decided that the two girls were cute but not overly bright.

"And what's your pleasure, Miss Quick?" I asked, trying

to get back into the action.

"Oh, nothing please, sir. I'm off now in a sec for Mr. Lennon is correct. I'm only a mere typing pool girl who has to catch me bus back to North John Street."

"I never had the chance to chat with you or to ask you out."

"Oh my word," she gulped.

"Don't get embarrassed Leslie. Just give me a brief try at least. One time should be enough to prove my merit," I said working fast in hopes that some of Lennon's magic would work for me.

"You say you're a mate of John's?"

"I'll stand by him," cut in John.

Ha. I laughed to myself. So once again maybe I would be gaining a conquest simply because of my connections with John. In the very near future it would become a very common occurrence. I would learn to despise myself for my actions.

The girls ran off to catch their bus back to the office somewhere on North John Street. When they had gone John relaxed and became friendly.

"Well, I'm back to the Cavern to help the boys break down. Gerry and the Pacemakers work the night shift," said John, gulping his beer. "At least with this gig sometimes we're finished at one in the afternoon. It's ripping to have the day to ourselves. We feel much like schoolboys cutting class. What about yourself, Al? School out?"

"Yeah, it's the Christmas break so I'm a free man as well."

"Well, come on then and say 'hello' to the lads!"

I spent the day with John, Paul, George and Stu. I don't recall what we did, but I do recollect Stu voicing his loneliness for Germany and his girlfriend.

CHAPTER TWELVE

"Here it is, Gin," I said, handing her the reference form.

"Oh, such a sweetie you are, luv," she gushed, readily snatching up the reference.

I chose that moment to kiss her. When she twisted away after a reasonably long kiss I could see a look of growing irritation.

"Ah, be nice to me Gin," I begged.

"Never mind all that chat," yawned Gin with boredom. "Let's get to work. What pose do you want me in?"

"Do I have to spell it out for you?" I said with a silly smile.

"Stop it this instant or I'll leave immediately," she threatened. Despite her words she remained seated, brushing her hair with her fingers to tidy up for my picture.

"Just sit up straight and look natural," I answered lining up my pencils and readying my drawing paper.

Hoping Gin's superior beauty would finally inspire me to create a superior work, I took my pencil and began my task. I worked rapidly, absorbed in my work. I thought back to the time June Furlong did such a wonderful sketching job of John Lennon at the Life Session. June had been one of the most talented students I had come across at the Art College. But Stu still ranked as the best to come out of the school since I had arrived. My mind wandered to Lennon who, along with that silly Marsden, had talent as well, but in music not art. Lennon, more than Marsden, was a complete washout when it came to the visual arts. I'd say Gin Browne, barring my natural prejudices, ranked in my top 10 to 20% of my students. She was consistently good if not great.

"Don't be so quiet, Al."

"I'm lost in my thoughts."

"What's all the deep thought about? You look like you may be taking ill. Come to think of it, you've been gloomy all day and it's a real drag. Are you homesick or something explainable like that then?"

Outside of my apartment the snow began to fall over the city, covering the grim and grit of Liverpool with a powdery white blanket. I daydreamed about Lennon and the Beatles. Where would they be playing that night, I pondered? What time would they go on? Then I wondered at my own fixation with the Beatles. Suddenly I was almost overcome with the keen urge to toss away my failing artist tools and pick up a guitar and start a band. Finally I shook off the sensation with a shrug off my shoulders, for I realized that the Beatles had the stuff to be great while I, at best, was mired in my own mediocrity.

"Only a little depressed, that's all," I sighed.

"Can you say why, luv?" she asked gently.

"I know this may sound off the wall but today I'm feeling so untalented, and the feeling makes me feel guilty.

"You're not untalented, Al Moran," said Gin sharply. "You're a crackup teacher, as well as a decent artist and that's not to mention your writing. There's other books to be written by you, so don't forget that. Where's your head at anyways, lad?"

"I guess I'm comparing myself with the Beatles. I just have a feeling they're going to blast off to the Moon and be great like Mozart, Shakespeare, Leonardo and a handful of the immortals of that higher order. I only wish I could be one of them. Sure, I may have more talent than the average Joe, but what is my ability compared to them?"

"So you feel it too? I think it's like we're all being left behind. Ha! Many people in Liverpool feel something like that. But isn't it marvelous that it should happen among us? Soon the Beatles will be far beyond any of us and this dirty auld town. They'll belong to the world, then to the ages. I rather suppose we'll have to get used to the fact that the greatest achievement of our lives was in knowing the Beatles."

"Odd way of putting it, but it's true," I agreed.

For as long as I resided in the city of Liverpool I could never rid myself of the impression that the English of that hardscrabble port town had a fetish for sex in strange and uncomfortable positions. The knee trembler, a dreadfully ghoulish way of screwing with one's bottom snug against a warehouse building, may serve as a classic example. But perhaps it wasn't the Scouse fetish and only Ginny Browne who fancied awkward ways of lovemaking.

The snow continued to sprinkle across the city as Gin bid me to sit quietly on the couch as she slid up and down on my penis when we could have just as easily go to bed. When we finished she insisted upon staying on me as she inhaled on a cigarette.

"Your mates the Beatles will be off to Hamburg shortly," she said.

The sudden closeness of Ginny Browne and I widened at the close of 1961 but just as quickly narrowed as the winter of 1962 took off. Since she didn't have me for any classes and she avoided the campus cafeteria and Life Sessions, I had very little opportunity to see much of her. Whenever I did happen to run into her she always feigned disinterest. Even the news of a published story of mine in a large and well-known London detective magazine and the decent sales of my *American Expatriate Writers in England* failed to stir her attention in me. It did, however, give me a certain sense of satisfaction that I, too, was putting down something for the ages.

"Did you know the boys are cutting a record?" she asked, changing the topic from me to Lennon and the Beatles without batting an eyelash.

"No, I haven't," I confessed, pleased to hear the news but feeling more than a little rejected in the way she had so easily blown off news of my progress as a writer.

"Don't ask me for any details," she warned. "I only just heard the news myself."

Since Gin didn't have the details I decided to give Leslie Quick, my sometimes typist girlfriend, a call and invited her out to lunch. Leslie, like Gin, seemed to only want to talk about the Beatles.

"Say, Les, I'll pay for your lunch if you can give me the inside dope about the record the Beatles are cutting."

"I thought everybody knew about that," teased Leslie, happy to be on the inside with the Beatles instead of me.

"So clue me in, kid," I pleaded.

It was at the tail end of the lunch time special at the Cavern. The menu featured bacon sandwiches, coke and live music. That day Gerry and the Pacemakers were the third item on the bill of fare. Gerry Marsden and his musical mates, recently returned from Hamburg, were almost as popular as the Beatles.

"Actually I don't know much about it Al, except that they're putting down the song *My Bonnie* for a recording studio in Germany where they've been staying on these past few weeks. They're becoming the best British band over there. It's fab, eh?"

"I wasn't even aware that they had left England again."

"Oh, Al, you're so out of it these days. Everybody knows how the Beatles divide their time between here and there. All the bands are forever going back and forth to the continent. Gerry and his lot only just returned from Germany and they're already making plans to go back."

"Yeah, I guess I don't have the slightest idea as to what is going on around here."

"Read the papers, dear."

"Getting back to the Beatles, dear, which label are they recording for?"

"I don't have the foggiest, Al. But a label is a label."

Along with the rest of the lunchtime crowd climbing the steps for Matthew Street we felt sad to be leaving the rock n roll fun for the dull work routines for our collective realities.

"I wonder who's singing lead on the record, Lennon or McCartney?" I said out loud as we stepped into the gloom of the winter day.

"Neither of them are singing lead, mate," a young man behind me said. "Tony Sheridan will be the vocalist."

"Oh, Tony's a Liverpool feller, isn't he?" squealed Leslie. "He's almost as cute as Tommy Steele."

"Is this Tony Sheridan guy a new addition to the Beatles?" I asked the young man.

"Our Tony isn't the one for bands, he's a soloist. The Beatles are backing him up with their instruments. Maybe they'll do the backup vocals as well, but I really can't say. They're just sort of helping out Tony who's a good Liverpudlian boy like themselves."

"It's a start," I remarked, thinking to myself that *My Bonnie* didn't seem to be a standard Beatle tune. I felt a sharp let down.

"Oh, by the way Al, I know something else about the Beatles that you don't know," sang Leslie.

"So tell me, already."

"Stu Sutcliffe has left the band once and for all because he wants to devote his time completely to his painting, but if you ask me that German tart of his put the screws on him to give it up because she hates Lennon and McCartney."

"Well, that makes two pieces of good news for one day. You know, maybe I did hear rumors that Stu was considering packing it in," I said with sincerity as Leslie caught a bus for the typing pool and I caught one of my own for the Art College.

It was a couple of days after my luncheon date with Leslie that I came across a postcard from Lennon in the afternoon mail. The postmark was from West Germany. It came as a pleasant surprise for me to recognize Lennon's scribble sandwiched between advertisements for scholarly art journals and bills:

AL CAPONE MORAN OF CHICAGO REARED & ROARED—GO TO A RECORD SHOP TODAY-RIGHT NOW, HEARING ME? AND BUY A COPY OF MY*BONNIE* BY TONY SHERIDAN AND (GET THIS RIGHT, MATE) THE BEAT BROTHERS (REALLY US BEATLES). GERMANY IS OK. BACK TO LIVERPOOL SOON. STU IS STAYING HERE WITH HIS BRUSHES... THANKS TO YOU. ARE YOU HAPPY LITTLE STU TOOK YOUR BLOODY ADVICE? HOW'S GIN BROWN—EE? IS SHE MRS. MORAN— YET? HA!

LENNON

In the following days I asked around the Art College about this record of Lennon's nee Tony Sheridan and the Beat Brothers. Nobody on campus seemed to be aware of the recording except though vague rumors. I took the time to comb the various record shops in the town centre only to be told over and over again that the disc wasn't in stock.

One day I was inside of a large local furniture store looking for a lamp when by chance I noticed that the store also contained a rather large section for records. Entering this music department I was instantly bounced upon by a handsome well-dressed man who was seemingly all too eager to wait upon me.

"May I be of service to you, sir?" popped out a question in that polished, sophisticated English accent that one quickly learned to associate with the upper class public schools, hence the posh style.

"Maybe you can but I doubt it," I said with a smile.

"Oh despair not, sir," the man said with a charming mock dramatic air. "If we don't have it in stock we'd be more than happy to order it, for it is our keenest desire to serve the needs of all of our customers. Would it be an American record that you are seeking?"

"No, it isn't from America," I answered. "In fact, it's by a Liverpool beat band. I believe the record was put out by a small German label."

"What is a small label, if I may ask?"

"I mean that it was released by a small recording company."

"Very good, sir, that. I shall remember that in the future."

"I'm not even sure if the record has been released here in England."

"Do you recollect the title, sir?" asked the man, his voice soothing and concerned in a smooth effort to please. I was rather taken back at how anxious this young man, apparently wealthy, was to help me. I was flattered by his attention.

"Yes. The title is *My Bonnie*. It's a remake of the original classic."

The man's eyes lit up with instant recognition.

"And would that be a recording featuring Tony Sheridan and the Beat Brothers?"

"That's it!" I shouted. "Do you have it?"

"Not yet, I'm afraid, but I'm in the process of ordering several copies at this time. Oddly enough you're the seventh or eighth person who has requested this strange recording. Our aim is to satisfy the needs of all of our listeners. But isn't it strange how so many people have recently been seeking for the same rare number?"

"Maybe the song is catching on?"

"Excuse me for asking, but are you an American?"

"Yes, I am."

"Is this record catching on, as you call it, back in the States?" he asked with absorption.

"I have no idea about that because I have been living and working here in Liverpool these past few years. However, generally speaking, European musical acts don't catch on very well in America, but that may all change soon because the best scene here is incredible. I also believe that if any British rock n roll band can lead a British Invasion, as it were, of music into the American pop chart it would be the Beatles, or the Beat Brothers as they were called on the record. I'm not sure who Tony Sheridan is, but I think the Beatles are the ones to pay attention to in the very near future."

"What a good show! A British Invasion of Music spearheaded by the Beatles. Jolly good! The Beatles, you say? Sorry if I appear to be overly inquisitive, but the whole thing fascinates me beyond words. I'm not a follower of the pop charts, I regret to say. Nonetheless, these Beat Brothers intrigue me. I have also heard them referred to as the Beatles and the Silver Beatles. Sometimes I see it spelt with an 'a', other times with an 'e'. What the Beatles means is all beyond my reach, I'm afraid. I have also learned that they are a group of local lads who have apparently gone to West Germany where they have become a smashing success and that they will shortly return to England with a fortune."

"Yeah, they're Liverpudlians all right, but I'm not sure about the fortune part. I knew them before they took off for Hamburg, for two of them were students of mine at the Art College. I saw them before, during and after their sojourn in Germany, and I'm willing to attest that they have quickly evolved into a sensational club band."

"You say you've actually seen them perform....live...on a stage?" the man asked, a note of envy in his voice.

"Many times," I openly boasted. "I know them all personally as well. You see, John Lennon, the leader of the band, was a student of mine. They're all fine fellows."

"Art student, is it?" the man whispered with his lips pouted in reflection.

"John Lennon was a long-time student of mine. And Stu Sutcliffe, the bassist, was also at the college, but I believe Mr. Sutcliffe has recently retired from the band in order to go back to his studies."

"Are they here in Liverpool now and actually playing up upon a real stage in front of a live audience?" he asked like a little child in awe. By the way the man spoke it was obvious that he had never encountered a live rock n roll band before in the flesh. His voice sounded like he had a dreamlike vision of what the Beatles would be like in person.

"I think they're still over in Hamburg, but they'll be back in town soon enough. They play fairly regularly over at the Cavern, a tiny jazz club over on Matthew Street. Their noontime performance is just about the hottest thing in the Town Centre these days. The place is always packed with young people. The place really jumps!"

"I'd really like to see these fellows, the Beatles, for myself. They interest me terribly…in a professional way, really. I say, I wonder if you'd mind dreadfully going around this Cavern Club with me some noontime. I am available to see these Beatles anytime. I'd not know how to act if I went into the place by myself. I have never been the one for pubs and that sort of goings on."

For a moment I hesitated to respond. Then I agreed as I wondered how Lennon would behave when he saw me with this slick record shop salesman.

"I'll call you as soon as they arrive back in town," I promised.

"Oh, thank you very much sir. I know I must appear to

you to be awfully forward, but I'd like to discuss something with your student, Mr. Lennon. You're doing me a tremendous favor, and I'd like to return the favor by treating you to lunch at this Cavern place. How is the food there, by the way?"

I decided to be gracious and refrained from offering an honest opinion. Instead I answered, "No need for lunch. A couple of cokes ought to do it and make everything square between us."

"How terribly rude I have been…and amiss. I haven't properly introduced myself. My name is Brian Epstein and I'm the proprietor of this establishment. And your name is?"

"My name is Al Moran. My friends call me Al. I am happy to know you, Mr. Epstein."

"And you may call me Brian."

I shook hands with this man, never even remotely suspecting that one day in the near future he would be propelled to international fame as the genius behind the success of the Beatles, as well as several other top British acts, like Gerry and the Pacemakers, Herman's Hermits, Sheila Black and Lulu. At that time I was also unaware that perhaps I coined the term "British Invasion."

CHAPTER THIRTEEN

I arrived at the Cavern Club a few minutes before noon to find Brian Epstein already glued up with the waiting modish crowd. Brian, clad in yet another stylish and expensive suit, was sticking out all over the place among the gathering of typists, shop clerks and other working lads and lasses. I momentarily regretted not having warned Brian against dressing up so posh and formal.

"Al!" he called out loudly in that shy but friendly fashion of his. I noticed that a few people turned to look at the owner of the public school drawl.

"It is a pleasure to you again," I said

We shook hands like old friends.

"Al, I'd like for you to meet my personal assistant, Mr. Taylor," said Brian, introducing me to a young man lurking behind him.

"That's Alistair," corrected the man as we shook hands.

I felt more than a little awkward as I pushed for a table with two toffs in tow. The nosey eyes of class-conscious England and working class Liverpool intensified my feelings. I felt some relief when Brian was able to order lunch without difficulty from a true scouser waitress. However, my apprehension quickly returned once the Beatles ran up on the stage to a large clamor, for I wasn't sure how the sensitive Mr. Epstein would react to the dynamic charge of rock n roll. Immediately the sexual sparks began to crackle among the young women in the show. Mr. Epstein sparks crackled not so far behind. His eyes literally leaped from their sockets when the four leather-cladded boys started their gig. Large beads of perspiration soon dotted his forehead. I was afraid he'd faint from overexcitement.

My Bonnie was sunk as far as this Liverpudlian record dealer was concerned. To hell with Tony Sheridan and the Beat

Brothers! It was the Beatles playing original Beatle numbers in a Beatle style that he was grooving to.

"Maybe these chaps have something here, Al!" Brian shouted into my ears between numbers.

After one or two more numbers Brian shouted again, "My word, they have some sort of animal magnetism about them that will surely elicit attention."

Only a few moments later he virtually sobbed, "Smashing, utterly smashing!"

And toward the end of the noontime performance Brian concluded with, "They're going to the top, Al. You see it, don't you? Your Elvis Presley will have to watch his step with these lads snapping at his heels."

"You mean 'his boots'. Ha. But you're right, Brian."

"I want to manage them, Al. do you think they'd even be remotely interested in, say, an involvement with me on a professional level?"

"Well you know, I like those guys a lot, but they're a rowdy group of hooligans. Their last manager was Allan Williams and he didn't think too highly of their professionalism. In fact for all I know they may still be working for Mr. Williams."

"I've been informed that the lads have given your Mr. Williams the sack," threw in Alistair.

"Can you manage an introduction for me, old man? I must meet the John Lennon and the Beatles!"

"Brian, I have already passed on the word to one of the waitresses that you're among the audience," announced Alistair, proud of his initiate.

"Oh, are you positive that was the correct thing to do Alistair?" said Brian shrilly. "What do you think Al?"

"It can't hurt, Brian," I assured him. "They're disrespectful guys but they're harmless. There's no cause to be frightened."

He wasn't interested in what I was saying.

"I'd be forever in your debt, old boy if you could sort of smooth things over between myself and the Beatles."

It was almost at that precise moment when Lennon took the opportunity to snarl his now famous putdown at a group of businessmen who were making quite a bit of noise at that table close to the state (I'm still not sure if he was talking over their heads and directing his comments to Brian, Alistair and myself).

"Shirrup, you with the suits on!"

Since the building was about to crack apart from the noise the Beatles were making, Lennon's insult directed at the toffs went over big with the factory lads and filing clerks, whose roaring laughter nearly demolished the building. It appeared that even at that early date there were those who were fashioning John as a working class hero. Laughter resounded in the tiny underground club.

Instead of the nasty remark insulting Brian, as prototypical man in a gray flannel suit, it only stimulated him further in a sensual way.

"Cheeky as well as musical, the naughty rascal," sputtered Brian, whose body was literally vibrating with ecstasy. It was at that moment that it dawned upon me that this Brian Epstein was a homosexual.

Like most products of the repressed forties and fifties I had an immediate reaction of disgust and contempt. Fortunately my more laid back Chicago Old Towne days had gone a long ways in tempering my feelings, and I was able to instantly come to terms with the man's sexual orientation. Perhaps at a deeper level I was aware that I, too, heterosexual as I am, was also turned on in a strong sexual way by the Beatles music…exactly in the same way that the teens in the Cavern and the art students and the sailors in Hamburg were turned on. I resolved then and there to be tolerant towards Brian, for he did seem a decent fellow for all that and besides, he shared a passion with me for the Beatles. Even after I silently accepted Brian I was still debating myself whether I should introduce the lads or not, for I damned well knew that Lennon would take off after this harmless queer in the suit.

My dilemma was magically lifted when George Harrison unexpected announced into his microphone, "We have a special visitor today, Mr. Brian Epstein of Epstein and Son Record Store. How's a polite round of applause for Mr. Epstein?"

As the absent-mindedly and half-hearted handclaps crackled around us both Brian and I exchanged wide-eyed looks.

"Looks like they received the message," said Alistair.

"Do you suppose they expect me to speak to them today?" Brian asked in a small voice. "I mean, do they want to see me right now?"

"It couldn't hurt."

"But today? I wasn't expecting anything like this, really. Are you sure it's all right?" persisted Brian, rambling.

"They already know you're here," I reasoned, adding, "Maybe they're expecting you to contact them after their show."

"Oh, dear, I don't know what to do."

"Talk to them and have done with it," advised Alistair.

I showed my compliance with Mr. Taylor's wisdom by grabbing Brian by the arm and tugging him through the Cavern's throng to the dressing room area before he had the time to figure out how he could weasel his way out of seeing the boys. Before the Beatles even finished their last number the small section outside of the dressing room was swarming with eager girls ready to be selected (or neglected) by any one of the Beatles as they left the stage.

Because of the number of people milling around we couldn't advance any further. Then the Beatles came fighting their way through.

"Lennon!" I shouted. "It's me, Moran!"

Lennon didn't hear me as he was busy engaging in hand to hand combat with the mob, so I tried my luck with Harrison.

"George! It's me, Al!"

George turned his eyes my way and smiled when he saw me.

"Good to see you again, like, Professor Moran."

"I have to see you guys right away. It's urgent!"

As I was shouting George, Paul also caught sight of me and he yanked my arm as he plunged into the dressing room décor. I, in turn, yanked along the reluctant Brian Epstein. It was only when we all had cleared the door that Lennon noticed me.

"Hello, there, Al Capone! What's this, then? Trying to get me back into the Arty, are ye? Well, it won't' bloody well do you any good, sir. Even me auntie has given up hopes of me becoming a useful member of her society so I'm stuck here in rock n roll heaven for good."

"Be polite Johnny, we've a visitor," said Paul, nodding his head towards Brian.

"Hello, wot's that then, Al? Are you chasing posh chaps with dosh these days?" John said with a mean sneer.

Recognizing that Brian was perhaps somebody of importance Paul stuck out his hand and said, "Paul McCartney at your service, sir?"

"I'm pleased to meet you, Mr. McCartney. I'm Brian Epstein."

However, after the initial hearty handshake Paul completely ignored Brian, busying himself with the care of his bass. Odd as it may seem it was at that precise moment, with Paul tenderly caring for his bass, that I fully realized that there truly had been a turnover in the group. Paul was now the Beatles solo bassist, completely free of the inadequate Stu Sutcliffe. So it was true, Stu had left the band. I was pleased but sad.

"Stu is still in Germany, then," I asked John, who was also studiously ignoring the fidgeting Mr. Epstein.

"You've got your wish, Al. He's back to the canvases and brushed for good."

"Yeah...for our good," added Paul.

Stu was already part of the Beatles' past as far as the others were concerned, so I decided to refocus on the present and Mr. Epstein. Introductions turned out to be unnecessary.

"What brings Brian Epstein here?" asked George, half to me, half to Lennon with a mixture of politeness and rudeness.

"George, don't you know how these sort work? If they can smell the possibility of turning a quick profit or pocket a quid or two they're at your doorstep at the shake of a lamb's bank book. All smiles and handshakes, is it? Mr. Epstein of Epstein and Son," cut in Lennon.

"Is that so, Mr. Epstein?" asked George, who didn't have Lennon's sharpness but who was more than capable of wounding somebody.

I was appalled at what was going on between the boys and Brian. Were they giving Brian the business or taking the piss out of him, but attacking his Jewishness? I wasn't sure if John's remark was a general stab at men in business suits or if it was an overt anti-Semitic slam towards Brian's family. Or maybe it was the common attitude of working class Liverpool that John was echoing. I suppose it wasn't far removed from the sentiments of my own blue collar environment back in Chicago. Still, if John's opinion was that of the general local feeling I considered it vile, especially considering what the Nazis had attempted only a decade and a half before. I also knew that Liverpool, a longtime major commercial city in England, had a very large Jewish population that was known and despised for its enterprise.

"Why don't you hear him out first, Lennon, before you start acting like a scouser shithead," I snapped in what I hoped didn't sound like a jesting fashion. I wanted to show John I was ticked off at him.

"Ah, it really isn't important, Al, really," Brian desperately whispered into my ear, tugging at my coat sleeves like a frightened little boy who wants to go home.

The other Beatles turned to stare at their leader, curious as to how he would rip me to pieces for the affront. Lennon however, in a sudden reversal, said "So you're a friend of Al, are you, then, Mr. Epstein? You should have said so in the first place. Welcome you are, sir."

John Lennon shook hands with Brian Epstein, signaling the start of a relationship that would bring universal glory to five young men: Brian, John, Paul, George and…and…well, that's another story.

"I have a proposition to make to the Beatles," announced Brian grandly.

At the conclusion of that sentence, I made my exit. My departure was not only from the Cavern but also from Brian Epstein and the Beatles as well as Liverpool and England, for I had to return to America to help my family overcome the blow of the death of my father.

PART II: SUCCESS

CHAPTER FOURTEEN

I celebrated New Year's Eve of 1961 by sitting inside of a smoky imitation Irish pub on Roscoe Street with three of my brothers, Adam, Frank and Pete. We were four Irish bachelors gathered together to share our loneliness. It had been over three years since I had been together with my brothers and I was only with them now because I had returned to Chicago to see my mother through the crisis following my father's death. Being back a Chicago brought me no real joy, for my heart was still back in Liverpool.

Sitting over pints of Guinness Stout and shouting over the racket of the Irish sing along music, I tried to convince my brothers that my friends the Beatles would be the hottest thing in the musical world by the following New Year's Eve. My brothers, bored and cynical, only nodded their heads and changed the topic to the Cubs pitching staff.

My own personal history pales alongside that of the colorful myth of the Beatles and the rest of the British Invasion, so let it suffice to say that I spent the early part of 1962 teaching night classes at the University of Chicago and doing pick up substitute teaching in the public schools during the day. Although I usually felt too listless to write or draw much, I did make some progress with a book about American painters living abroad, like Whistler. I also started to come up with other ideas for books to follow up my first book. The winter dragged on.

Eventually I mustered up enough energy to write to the Liverpool Art College to see what my chances were of obtaining my old position. I really didn't have the heart to believe that I could ever regain the former position that I had grown accustomed to.

In March I was surprised to receive a short and rather

ungrammatical letter from George Harrison, who sent me his regrets concerning the passing away of my father. The letter concluded on an upbeat note.

It read:

BEATLES ARE HEADING BACK TO HAMBURG FOR A TWO MONTH ENGAGEMENT. THIS MUST BE OUR FOURTH OR FIFTH RETURN. OR IT SEEMS SO. OUR WAGES WILL BE GRANDER THAN IN THE PAST. MAYBE YOU CAN VISIT US THERE AS YOU DID IN THE PAST. WE HAD A SMASHING TIME WHEN YOU CAME, DIDN'T WE MATE. WE CAN PUT YOU UP LIKE BEFORE. HOPE YOU'RE KEEPING WELL.

GEORGE

I imagined George had gotten my address from Ginny Browne who had turned out to be my most regular correspondent from England.

After some hard thought Gin had decided to put off graduate school in America and give London a run for its money instead. She was currently in the big city working on her advanced degree in art history while working part time for an advertising firm.

In early May I received a brief but terrible postcard from Ginny.

DEAR AL,

DID YOU HEAR ABOUT LITTLE STU? HE PASSED AWAY IN APRIL. SOMETHING ABOUT A TUMOUR. WE'RE ALL CRUSHED!!! SUCH A TALENT TO BE WASTED SO EARLY. HE WAS THE BEST OF OUR LOT AT THE ARTY, WASN'T HE? WON'T YOU WRITE TO JOHNNY, LUV? I'M SURE HE'S HURT, NO MATTER

WHAT HE SAYS. HE LOVED STU LIKE A BROTHER.

I wrote to Lennon expressing my grief. I expected no reply. However, in early June my mailbox contained a postcard from Long John.

AL,

COME BACK TO LIDDYPOOL. THE BEATLES NEED YE, SON. STEAL THE DOSH IF YOU NEED TO. EPPY IS WORKING ON OUR BEHALF. RECORDING CONTRACT IS NOW IN SIGHT. SURELY THE POOL BEATS THE WINDY CHITTY. ALL IN ALL I MISS YOUR HOMESPUN YANKEE WAYS.

LENNON

Odd, John never mentioned the death of wee Stu, still it looked like the Beatles were coming closer to fulfilling my New Year's prediction.

The less I write about the Chicago scene at the time the better. My father wasn't the only thing that had died in Chicago recently, for the music world was sterile and bland. Nothing in Chicago could come close to the Mersey Beat. The folk music strumming over in Old Towne did do much more than remind me that there was a war a blazing in Vietnam. Besides, to me, folk music was something that belonged to the Wobblies, Pete Seeger, Woody Guthrie, the Dust Bowl and the Great Depression.

At about this time several of my hipper friends were crowing about a rough and ready folkie who hailed from the northern mining town of Hibbing, Minnesota by the name of Bob Dylan. Elsewhere Peter, Paul and Mary, Rambling Bob Elliot and the Kingston Trio were guitar strumming their audiences to greater social awareness. I suppose all these meaningful lyrics wailed in hillbilly twang had a powerful message, but it seemed so sexless and dull compared to what the Brits of Liverpool were playing. Folk music wasn't giving anybody a hard on, like the Beatles. Then, too, I suppose that the folk sound was something estimable compared to the beach music and surfing sound that was flooding the States from the California coast. Even as early as 1963 I was 100% certain America would lose the musical battle with Britain if we couldn't come up with anything meatier than Jan & Dean and the Beach Boys.

Finally, in the early days of July, I received a letter from the Art College of Liverpool confirming for me starting with the upcoming autumn term. By early August, I was back on board a ship heading back to merry ole England and my old life at the Liverpool Art College.

CHAPTER FIFTEEN

It was a lovely blue English autumn day in October. I was unpacking my bags and trying to harmonize my grubby Gamier Terrace flat. Consciously I wanted to fix my place up to resemble the first place I inhabited in Liverpool.

I had only been in Liverpool for a few weeks and the new term had only just begun. I hadn't wanted to be bothered until I had found a place and had set myself up, so I hadn't contacted anybody while I lived in a bed and breakfast and went hunting for suitable digs. I had also wanted to be alone for a few weeks in order to let the surface of Liverpool sink back into my spirit before I attempted to get back into the swing of things. There had been nobody to greet me at the Lime Street Station. It was okay. I had grown accustomed to my solitude. I had opened up a bottle of Bass Ale to toast my return to the land I loved.

The first few weeks of the term had gone along smoothly enough as I went through the process of learning students names and impressing them with my Yankee teaching methods. Nonetheless, I stuck closely to the Arty, not bothering to contact old acquaintances. It seemed like all the students at the Arty were new and as I didn't establish very close contact with them, it appeared I had lost contact with all of my previous students. I told myself that I needed time to readjust to England after my recent unhappy stint back home.

It was a lovely but lonely autumn evening and I was nursing a bottle of lager while listening to the radio. I was only half-listening to the blab of the posh, pseudo-hip London DJ until his words caught my attention.

"Well ladies and ladies, you all thought Liverpool was only the northern port city that is home to all those funny talking dancehall comics and unemployed scousers, but here's a new twist for you all…no pun intended…so let's all listen to what the North has to offer us Cockneys here in the South. I think you're really going to like this one."

Love love me do

You know I love you

So please love me do, woo ho

Love me do

"It's the Beatles!" I hollered at my bottle of beer. I immediately turned up the volume to find out whose voice or instruments I could make out.

Yes it was easy to hear that Paul was the lead vocalist. I clearly recognized George's style of guitar playing. And surely that was John on harmonica and backup vocals. The drumbeat was strong and steady. Was that Pete Best doing the drumming, I wondered? Nah, didn't Ginny write and tell me Peter had been 'drummed out' of the Beatles. It seemed that I recalled her writing something about George and Paul being in favor of hiring Ringo Starr, the drummer of Rory Storm and the Hurricanes. It all seemed so long ago and hearing the Beatles music again after over a year made me confused as to date and names. Opening another beer I remembered Gin writing to me about the boys cutting a record and that they had wanted Pete to step aside for Ringo for the session. At the time the news hadn't really sunk in as I assumed the recording session was another false alarm or perhaps a Mickey Mouse deal with another five and dime German label or some toss away situation like that. But now I was hearing something delightful, truly delightful right there on primetime radio. How much Brian Epstein must have accomplished in one year's time, I marveled.

When the song cut its last groove the Disc Jockey blurted, "So there it is, kiddies The Beatles hail from the old port city of Liverpool itself. Did you like it, eh? As for myself I'm not too much of a staid Southerner to admit that I love it. Good show lads! Later on in the hours I'll be playing the flip side to *Love Me*

Do. It's a sweet little number entitled *PS I Love You.* Ladies, you'll love it. Laddies, you'll wish you'd written it yourself. That reminds me that both sides of this record are original songs written and sung by the Beatles. Yes, that's it: the Beatles! These young scousers can write their own songs, thank you very much. No Yanks involved in it all. Britain is beginning to rock to its own beat. That also reminds me to invite you, one and all, to get on the telephone and express your thoughts concerning the fantastic beat group from Liverpool. It's the BEATLES. Or is the BEAT ALL? I think these lads are going to beat all the other to the top!"

I was so excited over hearing the Beatles on the radio that I gulped down the rest of my beer and decided to end my self-imposed isolation by going to the Cavern to see if they were playing there that night. Once again I was feeling an excitement about life. This feeling had been absent for months. I only wished that I could be a Beatle. Well, no matter. However, before taking off for the Cavern I decided to sit tight until the flip side of the Beatles' disc was played. As I waited I recalled listening to *Love Me Do* in the past. They had played a harsh, rawer version in their Hamburg days. Needless to say, the recording had a slicker and smoother sound compared to the raunchy and randy one they had in the Rathscellar.

I didn't have to wait long for the flip side to be spun. From the opening melody I immediately recognized *PS I Love You,* an old standard of Paul. Once again the song had been reworked and remodeled. All sorts of things ran through my head as the song rushed by and the airwaves were once again taken over by an endless stream of commercials, dull American pop tunes and the worn out quips of the mouthy DJ.

Only the excited voices of the girls calling to rave about the Beatles kept me glued to the wireless. How was London reacting to the Beatles? From the sounds of it, great! Only one caller, a teenage girl with a prematurely aged posh accent, phoned in disapproval of the Beatles. It seemed the young lady preferred some Cockney group by the decidedly bland name of the Dave Clark Five to the Beatles of Liverpool.

I made my way over to Matthew Street only to find the Cavern too crowded to enter.

"Are the Beatles playing tonight, mate?" I asked one of the teenage blokes hanging around in the street outside of the club.

"That they are indeed, mate," returned the youngster, giving his friends a broad wink.

"And there's no getting in there, guv. The place is crowded with birds," put in one of the friends.

I contented myself with sitting inside of a pub down the street a ways from the Cavern. It was the same local where Lennon had sent Leslie to summon me to. I half-hoped that the Beatles would drop into the place before the night was finished. I was happy just to be close to the action.

"Pint of Guinness, please," I called out for my standard drink.

I waited until the pub was just about ready to close up for the night when who should walk into the place but Lennon and McCartney. Of course the lads were accompanied by two girls. The foursome were sweating profusely, but they were bubbling over with joy.

"Here they are now!" I called out from my bar stool, a little worse for wear from the drinking. "It's those famous recording artists, the Beatles!"

"Hello, Dr. Moran!" exclaimed Paul, rushing over to shake my hand and slap me on the back.

"Hey, Paul, I loved the record. I just heard both sides of your single on a London station. You all sounded great!"

"It is smashing, eh?" agreed Paul.

"All the callers were going crazy over it."

"A record is all that was wanted for the Cockneys to pay

attention to us," said Paul sagely.

Lennon, appearing to be happy to see me but trying to act aloof, finally came over and shook my hand. In a flash he deftly chugged the rest of my pint.

"So you're back then, Al?"

"Chicago's dead nowadays. Liverpool is where it's at for me. Besides they came across and offered me my old job back at the Arty. That was swell of them."

"You were bloody popular there mate and the kids wanted you back, I should think. But say, how long have you been back then?"

"I have only been back two or three weeks"

"And you haven't been around to see the Beatles? Shame on you sir," scolded Paul. I noted that the way he pronounced the word "Beatles" he made it sound like a sacred institution.

"Sure, Paul, the man has better things to do than to hang around with the likes of a lot of longhairs like us," sassed Lennon.

"That's the ticket, John," I joked back. "At any rate, I have been busy getting resettled here."

"And busy chasing after Ginny Browne, eh?" sniffed John, adding with a smile, "And how is she, then?"

"I haven't seen her yet," I sadly admitted. "She's in London these days."

"Careful, son, or you'll lose that one to a posh Cockney stockbroker if you're not careful."

As I ordered one last round for the lot of them, it dawned upon me that the boys had undergone a considerable change since I had encountered them last. And what a change it was! Gone were the greased back Elvis hairstyles. Now their locks were longer than before, but it was professionally styled and was neatly combed forward over their ears and across their foreheads. It worried me that their haircuts appeared rather feminine. Gone too were the leather jackets, tattered blue jeans and dirty tennis shoes. The two Beatles wore matching gray collarless suits and smartly polished boots with high heels. The punk days were long behind them now, replaced by a look that was a strange cross between the art student crowd and the futuristic mod look.

"I dig your wild new look. It's out of this world."

"Right trendy, eh?" laughed Paul, never the one to be embarrassed for looking sharp.

"It's the Eppy doing," complained John.

"Do I know this Eppy? Is she some girl?"

The boys chuckled over my questions.

"Could be that," giggled Paul, refusing to say more.

"Eppy is Epstein. You know bloody Brian Epstein," hooted John.

"After all, Al, you introduced him to us," noted Paul.

"I know that that Epstein. But I can't imagine the likes of that shy gentleman changing the likes and looks of the Beatles."

"He got us a recording contract with a major label, so we let him have his way and let him buy us the near gear," explained Paul, sipping on his pint and turning his attention back to the girl on his arm. Same old Paul, I said to myself.

"Eppy knows his numbers and percentages, so we thought he knew best about marketing us to the world. However, we didn't realize at the time what we were letting ourselves into. He has us all regularly taking baths and changing our socks, but he'll never get to where he can change our music," cracked John, uneasy in his mind despite his attitude. I wondered if John felt guilty at having to compromise with the real world in order to become successful.

Looking at John and Paul chatting up their dates I could see the gulf that lay between them. The Paul of the Beatles was an image to be molded to suit the wind that was blowing in the direction of money, women and fame. On the other hand, John no doubt saw the Beatles as a voice of protest, one that could change the wind's direction.

"Showbiz is showbiz," I said pointlessly.

"The Beatles aren't concerned about showbiz," barked John.

"Al, sorry about the gaffer," cut in Paul.

"Sorry about the father as well, mate," John tossed over his shoulder as he turned to his date.

"Then it was pub closing time."

"I guess I'll shuffle off to Buffalo," I announced.

"Can you sit for lunch and a chat with me tomorrow?" asked John.

We agreed upon a time and a place and then I went home alone.

CHAPTER SIXTEEN

"Can you catch the bill today, Al?" asked John with his mouthful of food and a moocher smile playing on his lips.

"Now that you're a hot shot recording artist one would think that you'd fork out the dough for a change," I retorted with my bastardly smile.

"If it's too dear for your teacher's pay envelope then it looks like it's the kitchen for the likes of us. Do you fancy scrubbing a pot, mate?"

"So you're still skint?"

"But beautiful."

"Sod it, Lennon, it looks like it's my treat again. Well, I'm glad to see you anyways."

"Glad all over," quipped John, referring to another song on the wireless by a Cockney band. "And here's the waitress just now with the bill. Pay the poor dear, Uncle Albert."

I made good for the check, knowing Lennon was taking advantage of me again and not minding it all.

"Mr. Epstein should work on your mooching ways, John. Still I must admit that I missed you all the same. Man, I even missed Liverpool and the Arty."

"Hard to believe you'd cotton to Liverpool over Chicago. What was wrong there? Why back to the Pool of all places? This ain't your natural like habitat. Fucking Liverpool died in 1890, make no mistake there guv. There's nothing here but us scousers, the dole, and the rotting warehouses."

"Shoot man, I don't know why I came back myself. Maybe I had gotten used to the Pool, the Arty, the Merseyside, my friends, you guys, the Beatles and…Ginny Browne. Chicago didn't seem like home to me anymore. I was lost there."

"Me, I can't wait to make tracks from all of this: the Pool, the Arty, the Merseyside, and the whole lot of it. I think Paul and George feel the same way as I do. Old Georgie told his parents in no uncertain terms that he'll never return to the Inny or any other school for that matter. Only Paulie likes the Pool a little bit. It's his big family, you know he has a big family and clannish in the old Irish way. Me, I have nobody here but me Auntie and a few relations. No Mum or Da or such. Nah, I hate this bloody place. Me parents did me a wrong turn by having me here. And then me father buggered off and me Mum died, so now I'm all alone. By the way, what was your father like? Maybe you told me once but I have forgotten."

"Ah, he was just a quiet blue collar guy. He was a family man, a church going Irish Catholic, a Democrat, a laborer and all that. I liked him well enough. We never really talked much, but we had no quarrel."

"Did he drink...I mean really drink?"

"He rarely took a drink. He nursed a few cans of beer on the weekends. He liked one or two Irish whiskies on St. Patrick's Day. No, he didn't drink much."

"Did he have any women hanging about? Huh? And did he work steady, like? Did he always stay at home nights? Did he love you old mum?"

"Man, so many questions," I laughed, not really minding John's nosiness. "He wasn't really a very exciting person or anything, so I have no horror stories about him. He was always home and I assumed he loved my mother."

"Me da, Alf was his name, was a ship's cook. Maybe I told you as much before. He was an Irish rover with a fair singing voice himself, but with no sense in him at all. He liked a bit of fun, that one. We lost sight of him years ago. Maybe the bastard died at sea for all we know. But we rather suspect he headed out to New Zealand. He'll turn up directly if his nose catches a whiff of my success."

"Do you miss him at all?"

"I have never missed him. I put no store by that crap! Me Mum's husband, Twitchy, or Allan Jones by real name, wasn't a bad sort really. He gave me two half-sisters, if that's what they're called, which is all right. They're nice kids. I was fond of me Mum. She's...well...gone...too. No need to talk about her again. Fucking truck ran her down right in front of me Auntie's house. Nothing we can do to undo it. Praying weren't no good, was it? Poor bugger driving had hit her before he even saw her. Fuck it all! Let's change the topic."

Our hands dug deeply in our pockets John Lennon and I headed down O'Ferrall Street.

"How is the record selling John?"

"Fab!"

"Excited about it?"

"Only a start, isn't it?"

"Don't be hard, be honest."

"Okay I suppose, I'm excited at times. At other times I get sick of hearing it and of being a rocker. All those girls screaming and wanting your cock only because they think it's special because it belongs to a rocker. What a complete drag. All of those foolish birds, the lot of 'em. But... yeah, yeah, yeah. I'm excited. It beats working down at the docks or being on the dole. And it beats the piss all out of the Arty."

"Are the Cockneys buying it down in London?"

"Eppy assures us that our record sales are brisk and we're surging upwards in the charts. But wait until our album *Please Please Me*, comes out, and then the Londoners will take notice. We'll show those Southerners what for! It'll be out in January."

"You're on the roll now, Beethoven."

"Roll over Beethoven! And here's a pub just now. Fancy a lager, mate? It's your money."

A couple of pints later and Lennon and I were serenading the afternoon drinkers with Beatle songs. John had pulled out his harmonica for musical accompaniment. I did my best to sing in key with him.

Last night I said these words to my girl

I know you never even try girl

Come on, come on, come on,

Please please me, oh yeah like I please you.

"Good sound, that," somebody said at the finish.

"Did you write that song, sir?" the bartender asked me.

Lennon and I roared.

"Will they buy it in America?" still another asked.

"Hell, yes! It sure beats that surfing music crap pouring out of California these days. And anything beats that dull folk music shit," I exclaimed.

"You think so, skin?" John asked brightly.

"Man, the Beatles have the excitement the music scene has been missing since Buddy Holly died in 1959, when his plane crashed in an Iowa cornfield."

"What's this Iowa again, then? Is it a city?"

"Iowa is an entire state."

"They should have burned down Iowa in honor of Buddy," declared John. "The Beatles will have to insist on not playing in Iowa when we're famous. At will teach the rotters. And we will be famous soon. If only that Jew Eppy doesn't fuck it up for us. We'd even forgive him being a faggot if he can sell us to the Yanks."

"You know Brian is a homosexual then?" I asked, letting John's anti-Semitic remark slide if only to avoid a confrontation.

"I should say we all knew from the start Al. Can't miss it, can you? From what we've heard he likes rough trade. You know, working class lads in black leather jackets, American sailors, darkies from the West Indies and such. I suppose he fancies any bloke who will fist him off with one hand and punch out with the other."

"Well, Brian has enough business acumen to recognize the abilities of the Beatles, and if anybody can promote that ability it will be him," I said, ordering fresh pints.

"Abilities, my arse! The faggot only recognizes the size of our penises hidden in our trousers. We reckon he fancies Paulie the best."

"I bet McCartney likes that," I cracked uneasily. "He's about the least homosexual man in England."

"Cyth, me gal, calls Paul the town bull."

"I hope Brian isn't pining away like a love sick teenager, for he does seem like a good guy for all that. Man, if I had known anything about managing rock n roll bands I would have taken the Beatles on myself. But I could have never opened the doors like Brian, so don't be so hard on him, even if he does happen to be a homosexual or Jewish. Anyways, if you're going to be international stars you must drop your regional prejudices."

"I could never see Al Moran being the manager of the Beatles! Ha! Stick to your oils, paint brushes and canvases, mate. It's your lot in life. Leave Eppy to us. And yes, he does behave rather like a lovesick teenager. And yeah, yeah, he pines. I encourage Paulie to lead him on a bit...for the good of the group. Unfortunately Paulie is having none of it. Reputation, you know."

"I find your attitude hard to believe," I said huffily feeling put out. "And why do you snort at the idea of me being the manager of the Beatles? I'm only making pub room talk."

"Allan Williams has come out of the woodwork claiming the Beatles are still under contract to him since he's discovered we're releasing an LP. We don't need any more contenders for the crown, do we? Besides, teaching is your lot in life, not rocking. Own up to it, son."

"Perhaps you're dead on about my lot in life, Lennon," I said coolly. "I can accept my fate. I must admit I do rather envy you and the Beatles because you're living your dreams. And I'll especially envy you guys if you become bigger than Elvis or Buddy Holly."

"We'll be bigger than those two put together," sneered John, waving his hand in dismissal. It was the first time I had ever heard him speak negatively of his gurus.

"And when you've accomplished that you'll have the pick of the lot as far as women go. You could even marry some famous movie star, like Bridget Bardot or Audrey Hepburn," I said with false enviousness in hopes to change John's sour mood.

However, my words backfired as John's gloom increased even more. "Fuck you Mora! Why don't you keep your filthy thoughts to yourself. Maybe I don't fancy my pick of the bloody lot of them! And I especially don't cotton to your movie stars."

"What's eating you kid?" I dared. "Since when have you become a saint concerning women?"

"I have become saint since I married Cynthia Powell, that's when."

"I had no idea," I gasped, almost dropping my drink. "I wouldn't have shagged you off like that if I had known. Sorry."

"We tied it up, all nice and legal, in the city court office recently. No fanfare, that. She's having a baby in the spring, mine you know. My baby, you see. I couldn't let the wee one arrive without an old man, could I? I'm not a right bastard like Alf. I couldn't run off and leave Cynthia with the mess to clean up, not after how Alf abandoned me and my mum during the war. Sod it, I married the poor lass and had done with it, see!"

"Good choice," I said softly. "It's not in my spirit to rid a guy on something like this. Once again I envy your luck."

"Thanks, mate."

I wanted to say something more that would make him feel

better about being married. I had always liked Cynthia, who was a sweet and kindly young woman. The new Mrs. Lennon was also very pretty, almost beautiful. She had sexy legs and fine blond hair, like a movie starlet. She had artistic talent too, having much more talent as a painter than John, judging from their work at the Arty. Then I began to feel bad knowing that Cynthia hand thrown away her brushes to become Mrs. Lennon. I wondered how easily the artistic temperament would surrender to the role of English housewife. I had no doubts about Cynthia being a good wife, it was Lennon who gave me grave misgivings.

"I haven't seen Cynthia around lately," I said, making talk.

"She's in hiding actually," said Lennon. "It's Brian's idea, that. He's afraid that me following will work her over if they discover she's me leading lady. Fans are like that sometimes, Al. They want to own yer soul. Sod it all, she's me wife and we can't even spend much time together. I suppose when the baby arrives it will be all the worse!"

"Even your fans should realize that you're old enough to be a husband and a father."

"Tell that one to fandom, especially Beatlemania fandom. We've created a bloody monster, we have. Dumb birds don't want any part of married rockers. Marriage isn't cool according to the rock n roll credo. Look how the fucking fans turned on Jerry Lee Lewis when he tied the knot. They had his balls up in fire before the last of the wedding cake had been eating, didn't they?"

"Didn't he marry his fourteen year old cousin? Maybe it was that that cost him his reputation and not his marriage per say."

"It was marriage."

"I think Brian is incorrect to hide the fact that you're married. One marriage in the Beatles can't hurt all that much. It may even give the group an air of respectability with the parents of the fans."

"That thought makes me sick, Al. And look Moran, I think bloody Eppy knows his business far more than you do."

"Calm down kid."

"Shove it up your jam butties."

"Back off, Jack."

"Give us a break, Al."

"I'm only an innocent bystander throwing in my two cents worth. Don't burn my balls off. I'm Jerry Lee Lewis, am I? Let me buy a few more pints and we'll change the fucking subject before we wind up in fist city. Dig?"

The alcohol was making me feel loose and fine. I didn't feel any mettle in me. However, the booze was having the opposite effect on Lennon, who was becoming sullen and surly by rapid stages.

"Sorry, Al, mate. I guess this mood is my fault. And the marriage and the baby are my fault as well. I didn't count on things turning out the way they are, fame and all included. But still…still I wonder what it all means. Why all the screaming from the birds! We're only just four average blokes strumming guitars and singing silly love songs. Big deal! It's going way beyond music. Is it magic?"

"Maybe it's because the Beatles are living everybody's fantasies. Every guy wants to play a guitar up on stage, sing jive, make a lot of money, shag all sorts of women, and to become famous for it. Being the Beatles sure beats teaching art or working the ferryboats. I'd give anything to be strumming a guitar or banging a drum. The Beatles are everybody's wet dream."

"Everybody had a wet dream. Nice line for a song, that."

"It's a partial explanation, maybe."

"Speaking of banging a drum, did you know we ditched Pete Best right before we began recording?"

"I've heard rumors to that affect," I replied. "Wasn't it ratty ditching Pete right when you were on the verge of making it big? It doesn't seem like a Beatle thing to do. And he was a solid enough drummer, so what gives?"

"He was never a Beatle really. He was only a fucking stand in until the right person came along and Ringo Starr just happened to be the right person. Oh Pete was an okay sort of chap, and we never hated him or such. We'll never forget how his Ma helped us get started off by setting gigs for us in her basement Casbah Club. A good thing, that. But Pete Best just wasn't the best man for the bestest Beatles. Ringo is the best! Pete never did quite fit with me, Paul or George."

"But the girls always took a shine to the handsome Peter. And he was a good drummer. Your sound was lousy before he came."

"Man, Al Capone Moran, you're lost in a haze. Ringo Starr, the former star drummer for Rory Storm's band, has taken over the drumming duties for the Beatles and he has put Pete in the past tense. If Pete's such a star drummer he'll hook up with another group directly, won't he? Anyways, do you know our Ringo or not? He's doing most of the drumming on our album. Surely you can at least see that he's better named than Pete at his best."

"Yeah, I knew Ringo from Hamburg and before. He's a four ace kind of guy. But is he the drummer Pete is? The fans will riot, I'm telling you."

"They did riot a while ago, but our Ringo won them over in the end with nothing worse to show for it than a black eye. And he's better than Best-er."

"Well, Lemon Lime, you'll know that better than I would," I quipped, adding, "but let's sing another."

On the spot John Lennon and I co-wrote a song we entitled *There's Nothing To Do*. Later on I noticed that the tune had the same melody as *Baby It Is You*. Lennon never did record our mutual effort.

Then John attempted to strike up a conversation about Ginny Browne, who he mentioned was back in town and doing artwork for the *Mersey Beat*, a local musical newspaper.

"The rag is put out by Bill Harry and Bob Walk. Do you know them? Anyways, your sweet Gin is working for them now."

"Is that right?" I feigned indifference, not going for the bait.

"And they're printing one of me own articles about the Beatles" John said proudly.

"I'll look for it," I slurred as the bartender called out, "Time!"

"Do that mate," said John as we shook hands.

CHAPTER SEVENTEEN

A few days after my piss up with John, I went to a bookstore near the Art College to purchase a copy of *The Mersey Beat*. The paper, a tiny thing made up of a few thin sheets of cheap paper, apparently contained all the inside scoop on the local pop scene, complete with progress reports of the most promising bands and the record chart. The editor was Bill Harry, another student from the Art College. I only knew him in passing.

I quickly found what I was searching for right on the front page, above the fold. John Lennon's *A Short Diversion on the Dubious Origins of the Beatles Translated from the John Lennon* was a cutesy, sometimes clever, many times contrived and always entertaining piece that was sprinkled with John's rhyming, misspellings and calculated puns. Later, when some critics argued about what Lennon would have done if he hadn't become a Beatle, it was often put forth that he would have either been a painter or a writer. I have no doubt in my mind that John's abilities as a painter were extremely limited. However, I'm not certain about his literary wares. Lennon's *Mersey Beat* article revealed a strong leaning toward satire. Perhaps he could have been a modern Jonathan Swift.

Lennon's later published works of poetry, *In His Own Write* and *A Spaniard in the Works*, bear out that he may have had some raw power as a scribbler. I've always wondered if he was capable of anything more substantial than mild satire, nursery rhymes, pornography, rock n roll journalism or merely ripping off Lewis Carroll.

1963 proved to be the year of the biggest turning point of the Beatles career in a career full of dramatic pivotal points, for it was the year the lads' fame rapidly spread from England across the Atlantic Ocean to reach the shores of America. As 1962 had been the year the Beatles' fame had chained out from Liverpool to London, 1963 saw this chaining out go out from England to my native land.

The *Please Please Me* album flooded the American pop charts with monster hits like *She Loves You* and *I Want to Hold Your Hand*. Leaping from America, these songs were soon on airwaves in Japan, Germany, Canada and the rest of the modern world.

Being a teacher in the Art College, probably the pop cultural hub of Liverpool, it was impossible to ignore the intense interest the students had in the Beatles. Because of his former attendance at the school, John easily became the most popular of the foursome amongst the students and, as a result, I attained an exalted status among the faculty become of my past connection with Lennon.

I was plagued by the same questions.

"What's John really like?"

"Did you know his mate, Stu?"

"Was Stu really a truly great painter, like they say?"

"Was John a good student? Did he have talent?"

"Is it true that John's married? Who's his wife?"

"Did you ever meet Paul McCartney? Was George sweet?"

"Who was nicer, Paul or George?"

"'Who was a better drummer, Ringo or Peter Best?"

"Were the lads jealous of Pete?"

"Do you still see John Lennon on a social basis?"

With all of the attention being given to the Beatles, I suppose it was extremely simple for my lectures in Western Art History to be taken over by informal chats of my personal history with John and the others. It was all too easy for me to allow my classes to become monologues. I didn't feel bad about allowing my duties and chores as a professor to fall into neglect as I became a celebrity in my own right. I was always quick to fall into the temptation of cashing in on my reputation as being John's 'favorite' former art professor. It's only now, years later that I feel any shame for my conduct.

I also took to regularly regaling a pub full of people with my accounts, tales stretched way beyond the realm of reality. How many of my yarns were based in reality, or in stout, I could have begun to tell. No doubt my most far out pub fable was that I had, at one time, come close to taking over the management of the Beatles before Brian edged me out. At times I almost began to believe the yarn and envy Brian Epstein's role. My second fish story was that I had chosen the life of an art scholar over the pleasures of worldly success. I began to accept my lies as facts. My bullshit grew more outlandish as Beatlemania grew all out of proportion to what the world had never witnessed before. The free pints and easy lays were initially my rewards for the Beatles' past.

"Are you a fairy then, Yank?" I was challenged.

"I beg your pardon."

"Only asking like and not looking for a punch up. No offense meant, Yank."

"No offense taken," I growled back over the top of my pint. Please explain your question, pal."

"Only this, mate, everybody in Merseyside knows that bloody Epstein is a bloody queer...except for his dear auld mother, maybe."

"That's Mr. Epstein's business, not mine."

"Well, all I can say mate is that it doesn't set well with me to see a bloody queers like Epstein and your bloody friends the Beatles stealing the show from real honest English lads like Rory Storm and Gerry Marsden. I'm only repeating the rumor I have heard. No harm meant. I only wondered if you were a fairy because you such a big mate of the Beatles."

"The Beatles aren't homosexual, even if Mr. Epstein

happens to be one."

"You may be right about the three of them, but I'll lay me quids down that that Lennon feller is a bloody queen bee. Right enough, that. Takes it up the back hole, he does."

"John Lennon happens to be married and his wife is expecting a child!" I explained in a defensive fashion.

"She's already had the baby, guv-nor," corrected the bartender. "The papers claim they named the lad Julian or some such dago name as that. Read it myself in the dailies, I did."

"Julian!" snapped the Beatle basher. "A right bloody faggot name is that if there ever was one. Anyways, even fairies can get married and have children so as to cover up their tracks."

"Do you have one shred of concrete evidence to prove that John Lennon is a homosexual?" I challenged, foolishly growing hot under the collar from the taunting. I should have known it was of no use to argue with a drunken Brit.

"What about this for evidence? Your man only recently snuck off to Spain alone with your Mr. Epstein. Is that proof enough? Everybody in Liverpool knows what a queer that Epstein is."

"You talk too much," I mumbled darkly.

"They were in Spain for two weeks. That must have been fourteen days of jolly good fun. Vacation, indeed! It's all over the town and in the papers, Guv."

It never made it to the papers how I smashed the Beatle hater in the mouth. I was becoming a violent drunk.

It was heading towards the end of the spring term of 1963, when I was standing at a bus stop in front of the Art College with the usual regiment of students, that Paul McCartney happened by. The moment Paul made his appearance all of the females in the vicinity literally began to swoon and the boys began to stare.

"Al!" Paul shouted, pumping my hand. It was the typical

McCartney glad hand style of treating one like a long lost favorite uncle. He was no longer the shrill-voiced high school punk who had buttoned his winter coat up to the top to hide his Inny uniform. Instead, now he was a prosperous musician who felt no uneasiness in greeting college professors on a first name basis.

I, on the other hand, turned red with embarrassment over the pleasure I felt shaking his hand and feeling privileged to say, "Paul, it's good to see you. You're looking well. How is your father doing?"

I had calculated my words, knowing that the assembled students would all rush away to tell the world about the Yankee professor who was a personal friend of the famous McCartney. I tried to act like it was quite natural for me to inquire about the great rocker's father. Yes, what could be more natural than for the Yank prof to ask his dear mate Paulie about how his dear auld Da was keeping?

"Have you heard *about it*, then?"

"Hear about what?" I asked, too vain to ask about the Beatles first.

"Me party, it's me twenty-first birthday. It is very important, like."

"Congratulations!" I said dumbly, patting his back.

"I'm after trying to tell you like, Al that we're having a party in honor of me at me Aunt Jin's place and we'd all love to see you there being sort of Johnny's favorite arty proffy from his dear ole college days."

"Sure I'll go Paul, I'd love to. Besides, I haven't seen John, George or Ringo in some time."

The names of the other Beatles caused an instant buzz from the nosey crowd.

"And I'd love to have you be there, seeing how you were one of our biggest fans back in those bad times when the Beatles played in strip joints…whoops, sorry…I mean, the physical art galleries…ha, and you saw us through our starving cornflake days in Hamburg, and so on, so please be there. Aunt Jin's place is over on Dina's Lane. Do you know it? Anyways, we'll send George around to collect you. Bring a date. The party will be smashing."

"By the way, how are John and…?"

Paul made a face and put his finger to his lips as a warning for me not to mention Cynthia's name.

"Who are you asking about, professor?"

"I mean John, George and Ringo. How are they keeping?"

"They're gear."

Paul gave a friendly wave to the gapping crowd as he took off down the street. Whereas I wondered if Lennon had the talent to be a successful writer I had no doubts in my mind that McCartney had the makings of an up and coming politician: conservative, labor or liberal.

Seated on the bus I was pulling out some pieces to grade when a pretty young coed of mine, Sandra Manson asked me in a timid but posh voice if she could sit next to me.

"It's about the lettering class," she began before rapidly shifting gears. "Actually that's a lie. I just wanted to know more about the Beatles. I heard you were one of the few instructors who could get along with John? We've heard you're the only one who ever passed him in your class and everybody knows how tough you are. Ha. Joke, that. And we all know you're a mate of John's. Well, I wanted to know if you're also a good friend of Paul's."

"All the Beatles are my friends."

"I think Paul is simply gorgeous."

"The German frauleins felt the same way," I noted.

"He ought not to have wasted his time with those Kraut whores. He should stick with one of his own kind, good and proper."

"Boys will be boys," I flustered.

"Perhaps," she said shortly.

"And he was a long ways from home," I said as an afterthought, knowing I was about ready to take advantage of this person only because of my thin friendship with the Beatles. But I also felt she was taking advantage of me.

"What's Paul really like, Dr. Moran? I bet he's the sweetest of the lot. Did he really invite you to his party? How gear! And how I envy your good fortune so," she gushed, her Anglo-Saxon eyes sparkling.

"Take me," she said simply. "I simply must meet Paul."

"I'll take you so long as you remember you're my date…at least this one time."

"Oh, I'll keep that in mind, luv."

CHAPTER EIGHTEEN

Paul McCartney's birthday party was conducted American style in the backyard of his Aunt Jin's house, where picnic tables, fold away chairs and plenty of beer and snacks took up the space. Somebody had rigged up an old hi-fi that played plenty of Beatles songs along with some old dance hall tunes to suit the tastes of Jim McCartney (Paul's dad) and the older aunts and uncles. The party could have been taken straight out of an episode of *Ozzie and Harriet*.

Sandra, my posh date, was dressed in her most expensive dress, looked completely out of place among the working class aunts and uncles who tried to be polite to her during the cross class mingling. To do her credit she didn't seem to mind if her efforts were not completely successful, for she had been in a state of high-pitched excitements since George Harrison had come to fetch us.

"Better forget this one, Dr. Moran," George whispered into my ears as an uncle handed us beers.

"Don't worry, George, I've already taken the precaution of sleeping with her before I lose her to one of you guys."

"You're a naughty boy, professor."

"I'll confess it to Father McKenzie the next time I go to confession."

"I didn't know you were such a devout Catholic."

"I think she's after Paul," I said nonchalantly, bracing myself for the coming loss. "Or any other Beatle she can get her hands on, so you should be careful George."

"Cheeky tart, her," he observed, quickly adding," Better not let Paul's Dot hear that sort of chat or she'll claw your bird's eyes out."

"Dot is a poor soul."

"Poor soul Paul, you mean," corrected George, hooting.

"I suppose Paul can handle any woman."

"Yes that. But me thinks our Paulie is thinking of Dear Dot less all the time and scouting for more birds. He's afraid the poor thing is getting daft notions since Cynthia hooked onto our John with the pregnant belly routine. Gosh, aren't the birds a terrible thing with their finger always itching for a ring."

"Cynthia's a good woman."

"And she is all that, Dr. Moran and more."

The backyard rapidly filled up with people as I, in turn, rapidly filled up on free beer and became drunk. Early in the course of the evening I bumped into Ringo Starr who introduced me to his latest, a dark, cute, bashful woman with a pixie style hairdo. I, who was now in a rather drunken haze, thought the woman's name sounded like Marie or Madeline. Later I would discover her name was Maureen. In time she would become Mrs. Starr.

Paul, the center of attention, was only worth a quick "Hello Al," as he rushed from group to group. Sandra, like a newly brought home puppy, tried to glue herself to her hero's heels after I introduced her to Paul. However, McCartney was used to dodging such faithful puppies and he was deftly able to lose her in the crowd. Soon he was too busy to pay any attention to her as he had his hands full, as it were, easy for him to keep my date at arm's length. Sandra, not to be put off, stayed as close as possible to Paul without raising his ire. I understood her desire to be close to one of the Beatles, but I felt pity for her all the same. To console myself for my loss I literally jumped into the lake and captured myself another mermaid, or more accurately, a barmaid by the name of Lillian Sayers, who was an equally drunk party-goer. I was just about to attach my lips to Lillian's when Ginny Browne said into my ear, "That's a fine way to act in a public place Professor Moran."

I pulled away from Lillian, who merely shrugged her

shoulders and twittered off to find another pair of lips.

"Ginny, it's good to see you."

"Al, do you know Bob Wooler, the famous local DJ and Emcee of the Cavern?" asked Gin, indicating her escort or date.

"Pleased to meet you," I said sticking out my hand. "I'm Dr. Albert Moran of the Art College."

We shook hands.

"Are you 'the' Dr. Moran?" Bob asked with mock awe.

"Ah, so you already know I'm Lennon's former and favorite art instructor," I answered with mock pride.

"Gin told me all about you," he replied, waving over another man. "Let me introduce you to Bill Harry, editor of *The Mersey Beat*."

"Hey you guys are doing a wizard job of spreading the word around about the Beatles and the other jive bands with the paper."

"I say, Professor Moran, maybe we can persuade you to write a piece for the *Mersey Beat* concerning your teaching experiences with John," suggested Bill. "It would have heaps of local appeal, especially with the younger set."

I wasn't able to follow up on the question because at that same moment Gerry Marsden, a grin across his mug, butted in.

"And our Professor can write. Has published a wee thing or two," said Gerry.

"Marsden!" I exclaimed, genuinely pleased to see him. "When are you coming back to the college so I can teach you enough so you can scratch out an honest living as an artist?"

Gerry, speaking in his usual open manner, laughed at my advice and shouted back at me, "Don't you read the papers, sir? I don't need to draw for me daily bread. According to the latest fan vote me band is second in popularity only to your blessed Beatles. And we're moving upwards at a frightful clip. By 1964 we'll be ready to wrestle the Beatles for control of the Liverpool jive scene."

"Not if you continue singing crap like *How Do You Do It?*" snorted Paul in passing, peeved at Gerry's party bravado.

"Didn't you and your mate Lennon write that one, Paul?" Gerry asked passively.

"Piss off, Marsden."

"No need to take that tone, whacker. And no need to be jealous on our account. Nobody doubts how high and mighty the Beatles are in Liverpool. You're the best and by far," cracked Gerry, not in the least put out by Paul's sourness.

"Too bleeding right, there, and we write our own bloody lyrics and music as well," boasted Paul, blowing off steam in an uncharacteristic fashion. I don't recall if McCartney was drunk or not. "We flat out turned down *How Do You Do It*. We only want to play our own songs. We reckon that when we get on in age and become too old to be rockers that Johnny and meself will earn our keep going the Tin Pan Alley route. Why I bet we'll be selling Gerry and the Pacemakers songs within the year."

"Regular Gilbert and Sullivans with long hair," threw in Bob Wooler who received a frosty look from Paul for his efforts.

"Gis us a break, Paul," cut in Marsden. "The Beatles do plenty of tunes from other people like Chuck Berry, Buddy, and Carl Perkins."

"Yeah, but none of those Yanks wrote rubbish like *How Do You Do It*," fumed Paul.

"It's your party, Paul," conceded Gerry, never missing a beat with that disarming smile of his.

"Cut the sermon, Paul," said George.

I began to feel queasy over the air of hostility that had descended upon the party. I was also feeling sore about the way Paul had trashed Gerry verbally. It was uncalled for.

"Right o. I'll fetch the ale instead," said Paul, making a

visible effort to lighten his demeanor.

"Getting pretty damn sensitive, the lot of 'em," Bob growled in my direction. I vaguely knew of Wooler from the local beat scene. He seemed like a decent enough guy who was doing one hell of a job promoting the Mersey Beat to the world by giving ample air time to the local groups on his popular radio show.

I wandered off to seek out Lennon, who was sitting all by himself, pint in hand, a glare frozen onto his face. When he was looking so fierce I was always more than a little reluctant about butting in. Sitting beside him was his wife Cynthia, who was for her part pale-faced and subdued.

"Hey, Lennon, do you need a refill?" I asked, draining my own pint and pointing towards the beer.

"If you have the strength to carry two, prof," he answered glumly.

"John, he's a professor of art at the Art College, not a prof! Can't you show anybody the proper respect they deserve?" Cynthia chided her husband.

"And can't you leave off with the nagging for a moment?" John returned the chiding.

The uncomfortable situation was quickly bypassed by an even more uncomfortable spot when Bob Wooler, a jokey look on his face, strolled over and called out in an obviously jesting voice, "Hey, Johnny, how was the honeymoon?"

Lennon and his bride exchanged uneasy glances before John snapped back at Bob, "The honeymoon is waiting until we can afford a decent one...if you must know."

"No, no, no, Lennon," cooed Bobby, treading on thin ice. "I don't mean the honeymoon with your wife. I mean the one you took in Spain with another person."

"Wot's that, then?"

"You know well what I'm on about Lennon. Stop messing

about. All of Liverpool knows you went off to Spain with your mate, Eppy the fairy."

In a flash Lennon leaped from his chair and sent Bob flying through the crowd with one solid blow to the jaw. The contest didn't stop there as John began to rain a hail of blows down upon the fallen DJ much to the astonishment of all gathered. Being the closest to the scene I was the first to grab Lennon. My forty or fifty pound advantage in bulk was no avail against Lennon's slender frame that was exploding with energy. He easily yanked away from my hold and went back to the task of mauling poor Bobby Wooler, who hadn't meant any real harm with his ill-timed beery teasing. I believe George was the next to jump into the fight. In mere seconds, Harrison's action was followed by a virtual army of mates and uncles who helped to pull John off of Bob.

Nearby Jim McCartney hissed, "Is that Lennon chap at it again? He's a bad sort, isn't he? Wished my son had his wits about him and kept himself clear of that bloke."

Lennon, against great odds, still didn't give up. In the tumble I received a clout on the nose by a still fighting mad Lennon, as the lot of us crumbled backwards to the ground. I instantly tasted the blood that streamed from my nose. It was my blood! However, nobody paid any attention to my wound, for Lennon was the first to regain his footing and he immediately raced off to the nearby shed. No doubt he was looking for some sort of tool to use as a weapon to clobber Bob Wooler some more. Maybe he wanted to clobber us all!

"I'll kill the fucker!" Lennon howled in a berserk fashion as he came dashing back swinging a shovel. Fortunately he was quickly overwhelmed by a flying wedge of mates and uncles. I could only watch helplessly as I tried to keep the blood from ruining my party clothes.

"Hey John, like you broke the professor's bloody nose," shouted George, waving his hand in front of John's glazed eyes and then pointing at me.

John, in the arms of several men began to visibly weaken as he came around to his senses. At that moment it began to dawn upon him the terrible scene he had caused with his temper.

"Maybe Dr. Moran will send to Chicago for some of Al Capone's mates to come hither and do ye in as well as the rest of us Liverpudlians," said Paul, mostly in jest. "I'd not blame him myself."

"You did his nose up something fierce like, mate," chirped in Ringo, a gutsy guy for all his lack of size. "You ruined his handsome Glenn Ford face, John. Al's a professor and all and liked by all sorts of birds and other students and such."

The nervous laughter somehow managed to relax John, who collapsed into somebody's arms and began to sob. Cynthia, who had watched everything terror struck, began to sob as well. Meanwhile a battered Bob Wooler was being helped to his feet by Aunt Jin and Jim McCartney.

"Are ye all right then, lad?" asked Aunt Jin.

"Can't ye see the poor chap is after dying on us, woman?" Jim barked at his sister.

"I weren't talking to you Jim McCartney, now was I?" Aunt Jin fought back. "And don't start in bickering with me until we get the lad off to the hospital."

"I'll take Bob meself," offered Paul, stepping in and becoming the director.

The birthday party half-heartily carried, but everybody drifted away except for the McCartney clan. I can't recall what happened to John or Cynthia. I, a towel to my nose, was given a ride back to my apartment by a fretting George. Oddly enough, Sandra sat by my side and held my free hand the entire way home.

"Don't worry any about having a broken nose, Dr. Moran," teased Sandra, "after all, it will have been broken by one of the great Beatles. One day maybe they'll write about it in a book and you'll be famous forever."

"There you go, Al," George said gently. "It's not so bad to have your honker broken if it's done by a famous rocker."

"Thanks a lot, you two," I said not without humor.

The remarks helped a bit at the time, but to this day I have always resented the fact that it has been recounted many times how John attacked Bob Wooler, but not one time have I read about my own infliction in the act. History is unfair.

In the morning I awoke with a bandaged nose and a raging hangover. Sandra, naked and lovely, massaged my sore head, cooing, "Does your nose pain you much, sweetie?"

"I'm dying, Sandra. Call me a priest!"

I wasn't kidding.

"Do you suppose the Beatles will ever invite us to another party?"

I was on the verge of telling her where to put it when the phone rang.

"Hey, Dr. Moran, I only called to see if you're still alive or what."

"George, I ought to shoot Lennon's nose off with a gun the next time I see him!" I shouted at Harrison through the receiver.

"Don't blame Johnny if you stuck your nose where it didn't belong," George said rather harshly.

"You Beatles always stick together," I noted glumly.

"And next to Ringo's your beak is the biggest in all of Liverpool, so you have to expect it to be whacked once in a while, mate."

"Look man, I'm dying in agony and you're busting my balls. Sure I have a banana for a nose but that's no excuse. Lennon was fucking out of his mind! Case closed!"

"More like a cucumber than a banana," retorted George,

refusing to condemn Lennon.

"Look kid, call me a doctor or call me a priest but don't call me a cucumber nose."

Harrison chuckled at that and said kindly, "I'll be over directly with some ice and some ale to nurse ye back to health. It will do you up quick, I reckon. Trust me, you'll live cowboy."

I hung up the phone and Sandra began to move in to help ease my pain. However, before she could act with kindness the phone began to ring again.

"Not a second time!" I fumed.

"Al Capone? Like, how's the snort? Ho, ho. Can you breathe through it, mate? Can you still stick it up a wet cunt? Ha, ha sorry. Actually Cynthia and I are worried right sick."

"Lennon," I could only get out.

"Will it cost me some dash to win you back, Al? I'll pay it gladly. I never meant to strike you Al, or Bob, for that matter. You were just there and so was he."

"Is your hangover as bad as mine, John?"

"Worse. And I deserve mine. Sorry, really Al. Don't drop me over this thing, mate. Don't you start to hate me over this crap. It was all a mistake."

"Nah, I don't hate you John, but I expect you to stand me a few pints to drown out my hurt feelings."

We both knew I was being more than generous.

"Done it is son. Cynthia's making you a ripping roast beef for supper tonight. We want you over. Bring a tart. Call Ginny Browne. She's only wasting her time with the artsy fartsy crowd. No offense meant, Al."

"I think I have a date actually," I said, smiling at Sandra, who rewarded me by beginning to give me a blow job.

"Bob's suing me. He's sore as hell with me. I cracked his ribs, teeth, and so on. He's all right, generally speaking. I mean he's not going to die. Actually he's not a bad sort, really. We had no quarrel before last night. But he had no call slagging me off about Brian in front of Cynthia."

"Offer to pay his medical expenses."

"Say, I'll collect you around eight. See you Chicago."

"That Lennon sure has trouble saying he's sorry," I said to a busy Sandra as I hung up the phone.

"First George and then John, you're a right popular bloke with the Beatles," Sandra gasped between gulps.

My reaction was checkmated by yet another ring.

"Al? Gin here! Are you okay, luv? It must hurt something terrible, poor thing. I saw it all, ye sweet thing. You're so brave. Your nose looked bad."

"The nose doesn't hurt nearly as bad as my head. I have a first class hangover," I said with a touch of bravado.

"It serves you right, Albert Moran. You and that lousy drinking. How Irish you are at times. And who was the tart? Oh, don't bother with a denial either. Own up to it, lad. She's definitely beneath you, son. Is she there now? I bet she is. She's from Wales, no doubt. The Welsh can be so crude. Well, tell her to take a hike and I'll come over and keep you company. I'll do you up right, sweetheart."

"Make it tomorrow, kid. I'm eating at John's tonight. And George is coming over right now with some beer first aid."

"I'll bring you some Whatney's Ale, luv."

"That will be great."

"And tell the bitch to tickle you beneath the balls. It drives you crazy. Ha."

"What about poor Bob Wooler. I mean, is he okay? He didn't do anything to warrant what John did."

"I agree. But I'm sure Brian Epstein will smooth things over in time. John's lucky Bob is a four ace guy and that he loves the Mersey Beat so much that he'll not put John behind bars where he belongs."

CHAPTER NINETEEN

These are excerpts from letters I received from the States.

November 1963

Al:

How's life in Liverpool? Have you heard of the big group from there called the Beatles? Some song called *I Wanna Hold Your Hand* is a hit on the radio. Saw them on the Jack Paar Show.

Your brother,

Peter

February 1964

Al:

Saw your Beatles on the Ed Sullivan Show. They're great! Everybody in America loves them except for the Greasers over on Roscoe Street. You know them?

Your brother,

Frank

March 1964

Al,

Hey, write an article about the Beatles and I'll send it to one of the local papers. If it's halfway decent I'm sure it will sell. The Cubs will be lousy this season.

Your brother,

Adam

March 1964

Al:

The Beatles play great music but what about all that hair? Give me Elvis any day of the week. The Beatles look like sissies. Bought *Meet the Beatles*. I like John's singing the best; at least I think it's John. They all look alike to me. Was John Lennon the one who was your student?

Your brother,

Johnny

PS

I got a pad over on Clark now. It's about a 10 minute walk to Wrigley Field.

April 1964

Son,

I told everybody at Church how you know the Beatles. Nobody can hardly believe it. You must be proud of your art student's success. Did you teach that nice Ringo? That's what I tell people. He doesn't seem too educated! That Paul is simply a living doll. I can listen to *Till There Was You* for hours on end. That George Harris is adorable as well. Is he married? Only kidding.

Love,

Mother

May 1964

Al:

Good news! I sold your article about the Liverpool Art College and your teaching experiences with Lennon and Marsden. Send more. It was brought in no time flat. I sent you a money order for eighty dollars. My fee was $20. Ha! Bring 'em back to Chicago with you, bud. We'll clean up on this old burg. Can you make it juicier? Girls! Booze!

Your brother, Adam

May 1964

Hey Moran,

The girls in Chi-town are all head over heels in love with the Beatles. Bring 'em around Addison Street some time and we'll have a blast.

Your pal,

J. McGurn

June 1964

Albert,

SCREW THE BEATLES!

Your nephew,

Dutch

June 1964

Uncle Al:

I'd like to s..w the Beatles. Ho, ho, ho.

Your niece,

Jeannie

June 1964

Dear Dr. Moran:

We understand that you're an intimate of the Beatles and we are interested in knowing if you're considering a full-length biographical study of them? Our firm would be interested in having the first look at any manuscript you wrote. Indeed, perhaps we can agree to terms for an advance.

Sincerely yours,

George Miller,

Publisher

The postcards and letters and telegrams piled up from the end of 1963 through the year of 1964. The Beatles first visit to the United States had amounted to a thunderous success, launching the famed British Invasion, which arguably, has continued to the time of this writing.

For this first time in my life my prediction abilities had paid off, for a year previously I had foretold of the impending success of the Beatles in my native land to anybody who would listen. Of course, I had never imagined the tremendous holds Beatlemania would have over America and for such a long period of time. Who did?

Three appearances on the *Ed Sullivan Show* had turned an entire nation Beatle crazy. Beatlemania, which had been a mere epidemic in Britain, had become full scale plague in the U. S. of A. Suddenly the Beatles had captured the top five slots on the BILLBOARD 100.

- SHE LOVES YOU
- TWIST AND SHOUT
- PLEASE PLEASE ME
- I SAW HER STANDING THERE
- I WANT TO HOLD YOUR HAND

Before the Rolling Stones came along a few months later in 1964, the Beatles had outdistanced everybody on the pop charts in the States and Britain by a longshot. America's top groups, like the Beach Boys, Jan & Dean, and the Four Seasons, seemed dated compared to Lennon and his gang.

The postcards I had received from my brother Adam and one Mr. George Miller, Publisher, where the opening signals for a minor touch of success for myself. The Beatles great splash had carried me along for a swim, alas, on a smaller scale.

On a rainy Liverpool afternoon in the winter of 1964 Ginny Browne alternatively serving me tea and preparing her own Beatles exclusive, complete with photo, entitled *Cavern Nites*.

"You should have a go at writing something about the lads," said Gin between sips. "After all, you know them as well as anybody in Liverpool."

"That isn't my style, Gin." I said slowly. "What I know stays with me."

However, I have to admit that Gin's suggestion was the seed that has blossomed into my current effort.

Oddly enough, it was at this time and quite independently of the Beatles, that I was able to peddle the manuscript of my second serious scholarly work. *American Expatriates in Europe*, my follow up to *American Expatriates in England*, was purchased for the less than princely sum of one hundred pounds by an austere and established British publishing house. The work never made the best seller list, but it was warmly welcomed by the critics and the literary establishment. The publication also led to a promotion at the Art College along with a tiny increase in salary.

A few weeks later, as a gentle spring breeze swept through my apartment, Ginny had another go at me about writing a book about the Beatles.

"You could make a pile of quid blowing the whistle on that lot."

"I don't want to cash in on them."

"Half of England is cashing in. Don't forget the thumping John gave you. Besides, the swine would love it if his Yankee hero wrote his biography."

"Ha," I said, laughing off the memory. "Anyways, I am not ready yet."

"When will you be ready?" she asked. "Bloody hell, you've been offered an advance by a Yankee book publishing company."

"Someday, I'll do it," I promised her. "Besides, I told George Miller, Publisher, I wasn't interested in writing a biography about the lads for him. Ginny, one day I'll fulfill my promise," I silently vowed. I'll write it all down no matter how painful the emotions are to me.

CHAPTER TWENTY

My days with the Beatles were just about over at this point, and things collapsed when Brian Epstein began shopping around for somebody to write a screenplay for the Beatles first feature-length film. The final nail was driven into the coffin when John Lennon came up with the brilliant of me putting pen to paper for the movie.

"I've never written a screenplay before," I argued with John over a pint of Guinness in a London nightclub called the Bag O'Neils when Lennon had first approached the subject. I was in town doing the night life scene as Lennon's guest. Later that night I would be introduced to Bill Wyman, bassist of the Rolling Stones, another English band that was seriously challenging the Beatles for supremacy. To my surprise Bill was a nice guy and highly intelligent. I recall Bill and I exchanging army stories, for he too had been in the military. I also remember Bill laughing until tears came to eyes whenever John made a snide remark about Mick Jagger.

"And we've never acted before, so that makes us even, son," countered John.

"Nobody wants to see the Beatles act, Lennon! They only want to see the Beatles period. Your movie will be like an American beach blanket bingo movie," I shot back.

"Sounds easy to write, what?"

"People only want to see the Beatles being the Beatles. A few songs, some dancing, and some other cute Beatle rubbish will more than satisfy the audience."

"So write it that way mate," challenged John.

Lennon had swayed me to his way of thinking before I had had the time to finish my first pint.

"I suppose I couldn't do worse than most of the crap they use in motion pictures."

"There you go, son," John egged me on.

"Even I have to be able to write better stuff than they use in those Frankie Avalon, Fabian and Bobby Rydell beach blanket movies."

"So do it, lad," encouraged John, "but leave out the bloody beach."

"I'll substitute the Mersey for the Pacific."

"You know as much about us as any other writer and you certainly write better than any fucking London hack from Grubb Street. I have no doubt ole Eppy will assign the worst possible scribbler to the task if we don't commission you first. It'll be a big help if you could take the charge onto yourself and come up with a halfway decent script for us to shoot."

"After this pint I'm off."

"What's the hurry, Al?"

"I have to locate a bookstore to track down a book or two on screenplay writing. I have absolutely no idea as to how to structure or organize a script for a film."

"Stick around and I'll clue you in on how to structure the bleeding thing. I have had a peek at a few BBC scripts lying about and I have a feel for it, and aren't I a bloody published author myself?"

I stayed and grew drunk with Lennon who had all sorts of zany and nutty ideas for the film project. Too bad most of his notions were too dirty for the cinema world of the middle Sixties. Perhaps Monty Python's Flying Circus, the colorful British comedy troupe that would become famous a few years later, could have used some of John's conceptions. I vaguely recall a scene that called for Ringo to use his large nose to send Bridget Bardot off on an orgasm. John didn't seem to care that the scene would never get by the censors. Besides, who would be interested in scenes like that save Ringo or Andy Warhol?

Bright and early the next morning I had just sat down to my typewriter when the phone began to ring. I was more than a little bit surprised when I recognized Brian Epstein's voice on the other end of the line.

"Sorry to disturb you, Albert, old boy, but John rang me up last night to inform me that you've decided to toil away at a little something for our feature film."

"I have already started work on the screenplay if the Beatles are interested," I lied, some foggy images popping into my head. "How's this for a scene? The lads, John, Paul and George are a rock n roll band in dire straits for a drummer. The three of them are walking past a monastery when they happen to hear the sound of the most beautiful drumming in the world. And guess what? The drummer turns out to be none other than Ringo, a monk, who spends his days tending a garden and praying while he spends his nights playing drums to Elvis records."

"Sounds...well ...promising," said Brian, cutting me off. "Type up something and send it directly to my London office. Remember, we're in a frightful hurry, so nothing fancy. Of course we're not after *War and Peace* or *Gone with the Wind*."

"I've already come up with the title. It's to be called *I Should Have Known Better*," I gushed and I should have known better than to get involved in such a hare-brained scheme.

"The film should be roughly ninety minutes long."

"Would there be any chance of getting me a written contract for my work?"

"Well, seeing how you're such good mates with the boys I hadn't thought a contract necessary," Brian drawled out slowly. "But...if you insist...I'll see what I can arrange."

Famous last words!

Needless to say, I never received a contract for the screenplay, but Brian Epstein perhaps out of his own pocket did send me a draft for fifty pounds to act as an incentive to help motivate me. I never received another farthing for my effort to write the script.

Nonetheless, I took the job seriously and I was almost at the very finish of the manuscript when I happened to pick up a newspaper to read an article that the Beatles were already halfway through their film production. I was devastated. More than being devastated I was absolutely furious at what I took to be a betrayal by my friends. In my mind I said goodbye to the box office profits, as well as the critical acclaim that I was assured of receiving. I also began to plan my goodbyes to the four guys who had stuck a knife into my back.

I immediately phoned Brain Epstein's office but I couldn't get past an inquisitive secretary who refused to put my phone call through in that stubborn British bulldog manner. I could have killed her.

"Tell Mr. Epstein that it's Dr. Moran!" I shouted frantically. "Tell him it's about the screenplay for the movie!"

"Oh, but Dr. Moran there's no need to trouble yourself about that because the Beatles have already employed Mr. Allun Owen as their writer."

"But that's my point exactly!" I roared, on the verge of hysterics. "Mr. Epstein hired me to write the script. I'll prove it to you if you'd like. Here, let me read part of it for you. You'll love it. It's the best scene in the movie."

The phone on the other end went click before I was able to read about John's fistfight with five or six members of a Scottish motorcycle gang or Paul's seduction of a millionaire lord's daughter, or George's vulgar performance on a stuffy BBC radio program. Good stuff, but alas, never to be filmed.

I was unable to track down Lennon or McCartney but I somehow managed to weasel George's London phone number from Mrs. Louise Harrison, George's kindly mother.

"Hello, George?"

"Yes?" I was surprised at such a cold response.

"It's me, Al Moran."

"Yeah?" he said again but with a little more warmth.

"What's this about Allun Owen writing the movie script?"

"Wot's this all about, then?"

"Lennon asked me to write a script for the Beatles, so I took on the job. Epstein even advanced me some money on account. I thought the job was mine so I've been busting my ass on it for weeks. What's the big idea?"

"Search me, mate?"

"Hell, my script is great stuff, George, really. You'll love it, I'm telling you man. It's probably better than anything that minor Welsh poet could ever write! Besides, it's full of good lines for you, man."

"I don't know a blooming thing about it, like really man. The screenwriting department belongs to Mr. Epstein. Like, he's our manager, isn't he? Take the piss out of him, not me. I only play the guitar."

"Man, this script of mine is the best thing that could ever happen to the Beatles. Tell that to Brian. Besides, John asked me to do it himself."

"Really Al, this doesn't concern me," George said firmly.

"Don't feed me that line Harrison!" I howled. "Lennon promised me the job, so don't back him up just because he's your mate...your king."

"If John promised you the job then you should shout at John," retorted George icily.

"You guys think you can step all over the little people," I roared, now completely out of control. The greed had taken a hold of me but good. I was damned if I was going to let them take this pot of gold away from me.

"You've gotten plenty out of us, mate," George answered back in a steely fashion. "You and all the so-called little people are making a bloody killing off of your association with us no matter how thin the link is. I have heard about the book you're planning to write about to fund your retirement years over in Ireland. You're a leech like the rest, Moran!"

"I've only written good things about you guys. I never wrote about what selfish shits you bastards really are!"

"Ah, don't bother me."

And the line went dead. My time in the lives of the Beatles was over.

From the Author

I question if the last line was completely correct; for there were more episodes involving the Fab Four and Al that had been put down on paper. However, Professor Albert Moran's manuscript was very fragmentary after this point and I have elected to cut out roughly seventy pages of text that didn't mesh well with the rest of the manuscript. I am not sure if my uncle intended to return to his work and to smooth-out the ending of his tale, or if he just couldn't come to emotional terms with what happened afterwards. I rather suspect the later than the former. He did make several startling claims that I found to be interesting reading but that were too jumbled and incoherent to include with the rest of the story. In spite of his dust-up with George Harrison on the phone, he asserted that he had appeared as one of the British bobbies who were chasing the Beatles around the streets of London in the final reel of the movie. Apparently he also scored a bit part in their follow-up movie *Help!* He portrayed one of Leo McKern's eastern henchmen. He devoted an entire chapter how he, John Lennon and a very young Jimi Hendrix made their way over to Belfast, Northern Ireland, where the trio was arrested by the Royal Ulster police for singing rebel songs on a street corner. The recognition of the great Beatles saved them all from a beating. There was a long and rambling account of Paul McCartney dropping in on him at the Liverpool Art College and making a guest appearance in one of his lecture halls.

Curiously my uncle never mentioned visiting the Farrell family in Kenosha, Wisconsin with his beautiful and wonderful wife, Ginny. We all loved her dearly because of her beauty, humor and wisdom. We all fought to sit next to her at the supper table, on the front porch and at Mass. We loved it when she cuddled up and kissed us with unabashed fondness. Truth be known, she was the first flesh and blood women who sparked my own sexual awareness. I will keep the details to myself if the reader doesn't object?

Returning to my uncle's manuscript, he went on to allege that he was working on a screenplay for the Beatles' Apple Corporation with the working title of *The Adventures of Frodo the Hobbit featuring the Beatles* when he received his pink slip. Oddly enough, it appeared that Ginny Browne was also working at the corporation at the same time. He accused her of spiking his coffee with LSD and having him fired when he had a bad trip. I find that unlikely. It may have just been my uncle trying to connect with the hippie generation of the late sixties. I did almost believe the part where he challenged Sean Connery to a fistfight when the Scottish actor from the James Bond film series put the hit on Gin in a swinging London night club. I had to chuckle to myself when the old boy stated outright that Paul McCartney had named his song *Uncle Albert* in his honor! Was it all Irish blarney or was it the truth? Knowing the Moran and Farrell family, I would reckon it is somewhere between fact and fiction! I would like to see my uncle's work published, so I avoided including anything that I considered too inflammatory even after all of these years. I slotted this note in here to serve as a bridge to the final postscript of Al Moran's memoir.

—Steven G. Farrell

POSTSCRIPT

It was a rainy day in late November of 1980 when I, along with a stunned world, heard the news of John Lennon's murder right outside of his very own New York City apartment building. At first I had wondered if his death had involved a woman, drugs or professional jealousy. I could only feel a sense of bafflement when I read that David Chapman, John's assassin, was a religious fanatic who bore John no grudge based in reality. Lennon's death left me feeling sad and empty. For years I nursed a little fantasy that one day we would be mates again. Then I grieved all over again in the opening days of the new century when my old mate George Harrison died from cancer. I bitterly regretted not having made my peace with him. George had become a deeply spiritual man during the course of his life, so I have always hoped that he knew that I still was fond of him.

*   *   *

The last time I encountered Ginny Brown was in October of 2005. She had married me back in 1965 but we had gone our separate ways by 1968. Since we were both Catholics, we had decided not to go through the painful process of divorce. Over the years we had kept in touch and on occasion we even rekindled our passions for one another. She had gone on to a very successful career as a photographer and journalist. She also had picked up plenty of work with the BBC as a screenplay doctor.

We had spent the day walking through the damp streets of Liverpool and enjoying the colors of the falling leaves. It was her idea to take a ferryboat ride across the Mersey River. Oddly enough, it was the first time the two of us had ever taken that ride together.

Somebody nearby had a radio blaring and we could hear the sounds of Gerry and the Pacemakers classic song *Ferry*

Across the Mersey. It was fitting to the occasion.

"I haven't heard that song in years," I remarked.

Ginny squeezed my hand and stared into my eyes. There was a smile on her lips, but I could see the sadness that lingered inside of her big brown eyes.

"Al, I'm sick."

"Why don't you come back to me now? We see it out together."

I wanted to say more but she put her finger to my lips and hushed me up. She leaned over and kissed me.

"I shall love you until the day I day, Ginny Browne Moran."

"I shall love you for all eternity, my husband."

"Come to me now."

She only smiled and shook her head.

Jennifer Colleen Browne Moran passed way in the early winter days of 2006. She was still an extremely beautiful woman well into her sixties. She left me a large legacy of British pounds that was in no way a replacement for her love. The bright colors of life were washed out forever in my eyes.

I refused to see her resting inside of her coffin within the Roman Catholic Metropolitan Cathedral of Christ the King until Gerry Marsden locked arms with me and forced me to go inside.

"Your Beatrice is waiting for you to say goodbye, Al, mate," Gerry said gently to me.

We went into the church for the funeral mass and I saw her for the last time. It was the death that buckled my Irish-American rebel knees for the rest of my days on earth. I looked and looked through the sea of faces until I found that of Paul McCartney. He turned and winked at me. I felt forgiveness all around.

*   *   *

Even after the death of Ginny, I still smiled, but not as wide as before. I still kissed female lips, but they never tasted as sweet. I still laughed, but the old roar was missing.

I have long since retired and my doctor lies to my face that I shall live well into the 21st century. I have long retained the cynical nature of my Irish and German peasant ancestors and I could tell when the wool was being pulled over my eyes. I don't count on seeing the flowers bloom again in the spring. My soul never left the Sixties. I sing over and over to myself the lyrics from an old Irish ballad, "it's nearly over now and I'm easy."

Although the past years have passed by all too swiftly, I still dream of Ginny, John, and of dear, dirty Liverpool, the crumbling port city perched upon the Mersey River that will be the final resting place for my Irish-Yankee bones. Looking back I feel blessed to have known the Beatles. I was a very lucky man!

Ma, set the table, for I'll be home soon with my lovely bride, Ginny. John, mind your manners. George, these are my brothers and sisters. My dad was a working man like yours. Where did Ginny get off to?

Ginny, Gin, G....

February 7th, 2009

Dear Uncle Adam,

Uncle Al was laid to rest today over here in his beloved England. I was surprised at the large turnout for the high mass said for the repose of his soul at St. Peter's Catholic Church. Father Ronald Putnam performed the holy sacrament. I looked and I looked and then I saw Paul McCartney sitting a few pews behind me. I'm not sure if he recognized the family resemblance, but he smiled and nodded in my direction. After the performance of the family tradition of the playing of the Irish bagpipes, the kindly priest who had chanted the final prayers over your brother's coffin introduced me to several people. I was surprised by the warmth and charm these worn-out and aging people of Liverpool greeted me with. Many of them had been students of Uncle Al during his many years at the art college. I met Bill Harry, Gerry Marsden and many others of the old Mersey Beat crowd.

"We all loved Al Moran," said a voice from behind me.

"That's very kind of you to say," I responded as I turned around.

Ringo Starr shook my hand with warmth.

"Liverpool loved him. The Beatles loved him. John Lennon loved him. Our Ginny loved him the most."

I said my final goodbyes to my uncle who now rested next to his beloved Ginny as the others drifted to the parish hall for the meal for the departed. I refused to cry because I felt I had reached the point of my life where the tears had been crushed out of me forever.

"On behalf of the Moran, Farrell, McNamara, Powers and Gleeson families, I want to wish you both a blessed journey to your next destination," I said softly to the two tombstones in front of me.

I could feel the very presence of the Mersey River rushing by only a few blocks away and then I began to cry softly over the stone and the story of Ginny and Al, my aunt and uncle.

I'll be flying back to Chicago in two days. Uncle Al's manuscript will be safely tucked away inside of my suitcase. I feel very privileged to carry *Mersey Boys* home.

Love to all

Steve

The Wandering Celt

About the Author

Steven G. Farrell is a Professor of Speech-Communication at Greenville Technical College in Greenville, South Carolina. *Farrell's Irish Papers* and *Bowery Ripper on the Loose* were both published by World Audience Publishers of New York City. Many of his articles, short stories and reviews have appeared on-line including *Mickey Machine Gun is Back (Crime)*, *Galloping Gallagher Deserves the Gallows (Talking Pictures)*, *Black and Green Smash Mouth (Irish-American Post)*, *Four Irish-American Hellcats (The Path)*, and *The Fighting Irish in Hollywood (Irish-American Cultural Institute)*. His play, *Boston Knuckles*, has appeared in *Audience*. Steven G. Farrell's novels include *Zen Babe (2008)* and *Liverpool Roared (2009)*. *Mersey Boys* is Professor Farrell's fifth published novel.

Made in the USA
Charleston, SC
11 May 2015